THE ELEVEN DAYS OF CHRISTMAS

JP Major

Published by JP Major, 2023.

This is a work of fiction. Similarities to real people, places, or events are entirely coincidental.

THE ELEVEN DAYS OF CHRISTMAS

First edition. November 17, 2023.

Copyright © 2023 JP Major.

Written by JP Major.

Chapter 34 123
Chapter 35 129
Chapter 36 131
Chapter 37 135
Chapter 38 138
Chapter 39 148
Chapter 40 156

Table of Contents

Chapter One 1
Chapter Two 5
Chapter Three 12
Chapter Four 15
Chapter Five 20
Chapter Six 22
Chapter Seven 29
Chapter Eight 30
Chapter Nine 34
Chapter Ten 37
Chapter Eleven 38
Chapter Twelve 4
Chapter Thirteen
Chapter Fourteen
Chapter Fifteen
Chapter Sixteen
Chapter Seventeen
Chapter Eighteen
Chapter 19
Chapter 20
Chapter 21
Chapter 22
Chapter 23
Chapter 24
Chapter 25
Chapter 26
Chapter 27
Chapter 28
Chapter 29
Chapter 30
Chapter 31
Chapter 32
Chapter 33

I appreciate that talking about the second book I've written (*The Huntrodds Coincidences* is still available in paperback and online) makes things sound a tad grander than is really the case. While family and friends have helped its progression from the metaphorical blank sheet of paper I stared at on 9 March 2022, to the final on-line grammatical run through that began in early October 2023, my story has not been edited by anyone who actually knows what they're doing!

However, it *is* the second book that I've written – and, in the words of Harry Worth, "I don't know why; but there it is."

(And in any event, I'm quite proud of the way it's turned out).

For those who make it through to the end – I thank you and hope you don't find too many mistakes.

For Lewis and Gill, who both know Ryelands Park in Lancaster well.

And Greig and Steve – we miss you both.

And Tim, Jean, Ira, Susie's grandmother, Andy, James (F), Will, Wendy, James (A), Nick, Jim, Christine, Jubber, Rob, Brian, Steve, Maria and Julie, despite, for all I know, none of you having the faintest idea what the main park in Lancashire's county town is called.

I appreciate it's a tad late, but I hope you don't mind me having incorporated your names into the tale on the following pages.

THE ELEVEN DAYS OF CHRISTMAS

Chapter One

Adam Nicola was sitting in the far windowless corner of the newsroom, attempting to make sense of what was on the other side of the cracked screen of the worst laptop in the office.

While he should have been hard at work for over an hour, he had instead spent the time less productively, fuming and cursing – in fairly equal measure – the *hot-desking* policy recently introduced by HR, and the non-appearance of the number 100 bus. The latter had resulted in his late arrival into the office and Hobson's choice of desks and IT equipment.

Adam was what many 1950s American crime writers would have lazily described as *a smart kid*. He'd left home in Bristol to study journalism in Wales and had come away with a BA (Hons). Sticking with the paperback vibe, he was *a good-lookin' kind of guy* who, given a captive audience, felt pretty confident at being able to win anyone over with his engaging wit and repartee. Alas, getting 19-year-old under graduates to eat out of your hand on campus and persuading the editor of *The Lancaster Star* to make you a junior copywriter are two extremely different things. His attempt, part way through the interview, to make his inquisitor laugh had been unwise. Indeed, the decision to try the whimsical, ice-breaking tale of a journalist sentenced to die on the gallows who, on hearing the executioner has run out of rope, says, "Well, I guess no noose is good news." almost sealed his fate before he'd started. But, as it happened on that day, a dozen or so weeks earlier, luck and timing were on his side.

His had been the last of eight mind-numbing interviews for the post of junior copywriter. Ffion Griffiths, Editor in Charge had endured seven interviews since seven thirty a.m. and much of the positivity and hope with which she had started that morning had taken a hit early on.

She'd reached the end of her check list of things to ask candidate number one and almost by rote threw in the usual closing question, asking if there was anything else he'd like to say. Fully expecting the traditional response of a bit of shoe shuffling and mumbling of "no, I don't think so", she made to stand up and bid him farewell. However, before she had the chance to say that she would let him know the outcome of his interview by the end of the week, he stood up and launched into what Ffion could only assume he felt would be a job-winning move by reciting a poorly scanned fifteen-stanza limerick involving a subeditor called Rollocks. Any chance of him securing employment had dissipated even before he'd introduced *Nantucket* into his party piece.

Not long into the next hopeful's *interrogation*, it became clear that this guy had never heard of the *Pulitzer Prize*. Now, Ms G was not under the misapprehension that any hack on her provincial paper was ever likely to come within a million headlines of this premier journalistic award, but hey, if you're going for an interview as a reporter, she thought you should at least feign *some* interest in the subject matter.

Her third applicant couldn't even spell Pulitzer, but at least, as she showed him out of the door somewhat earlier than planned, this meant she could get ahead of herself and squeeze in the next aspirant before lunch.

Alas, her little mealtime ruse was soon thwarted when numbers four and five skipped into the room, linked arm in arm, dressed in identical frocks covered in prints of tightly sharpened brown HP pencils and insisting on being dealt with together. Ffion had noticed earlier that there were twins on the shortlist and remembered being intrigued by the fact they had studied in both Perpignan and Rendsburg, two towns twinned with Lancaster. However, this odd double act (if the dramatic entrance was not enough, their predilection of answering every question on behalf of the other sister and, rather disconcertingly given they were [now] sitting next to each other, in the third person) soon dispelled any romantic notion this coincidence had first held. It also ensured they were - equally swiftly - removed from said list.

As she whooshed Tweedledee and Tweedledum out of the building, she thought she'd nip round the corner to her favourite deli for her favourite lunchtime meal, pastrami on rye (with a pickle on the side, obviously), diet coke and a bag of quavers. She hoped to eat this indulgence of food sitting perched on one of the high stools at the window facing out while watching *hoi polloi* of Lancaster go by. Unfortunately, it seemed that the entire *polloi* of Great John Street had chosen that very moment to pop into *Sally's Sarnies* ahead of her for their own ciabatta of choice and by the time Ffion had reached the counter it was too late to even contemplate eating in. Asking for it to be wrapped, she rushed straight back to the office thinking she might just have a quiet few moments left to herself before the next budding scribe arrived. Of course, no sooner had she stepped out of the lift than the sub editor announced – with a slightly wry smile that she made a mental note to admonish her on later - she had better get a wriggle-on as her "two o'clock" was already here. Of course he is, she cursed under her breath. Without breaking stride and leaving the untouched take-out on her secretary's desk, she strode into the meeting room, only to find that, unlike her, *Number Six* had not discarded his own meal and indeed was busy munching his way through a cheese and onion on white.

She thought surely – even if only by the law of averages – one of her last two hopefuls must come good, although it soon became apparent that despite her position on the list, candidate seven would not prove to be her lucky number. This one had, it seemed, two default responses, irrespective of what was being asked: no and yes (though not necessarily in that order). Even the most open of questions didn't manage to open her up.

When Mr Nicola was ushered in for the (thank St Francis de Sales, Ffion thought to herself) final interview of the day, Editor Griffiths was just about ready to give removing her eyes with the left-handed Osmiroid gold nibbed pen her father had given her the day she graduated from Cardiff Uni a go. We'll never know if Adam would have thought twice about carrying on with his little *no noose* quip had he been aware of his potential boss's then state of mind. Of course, he had no idea whatsoever and ahead he ploughed – and in such a state of total oblivion that he didn't even notice the interviewer's pen starting to strike continuous lines through his name at the head of the page on her clipboard.

It was about the time he reached his punch line that Ffion noticed two things jump out of the candidate's CV. At first, seeing his home address was in southwest England simply bolstered the ferocity with which she was obliterating his name on her note pad. (Her default position was to despise any English person she met on sight and, only if absolutely necessary, consider at a more leisurely pace whether there were any mitigating circumstances at all that might change that opinion). However, rather surprisingly – and at world record speed – said mitigation presented itself a few lines down the resume when she spotted that his degree was from Cardiff. Suddenly she was transported back to her hometown in the Welsh capital, recalling the happy days she spent at the university where, in 2005 she had become the first recipient of the first degree it had ever awarded.

When Adam responded to her question about the university's motto with an impressively articulated, *Gwirionedd Undod a Chytgord*, rather than offering the (rather loose) English translation, *Truth, Unity and Concord*, he was three quarters of the way to the finish line. When he managed the spelling of *Pulitzer* correctly – and doing so without even pausing to question why on earth she wanted to know - her decision was made: Mr Nicola was clearly the best of the bad bunch she'd waded through today. Admittedly the bar had been set pretty low by the previous seven candidates, but she felt, with a bit of luck, she could certainly do a great deal worse than employing *Boyo* here - and so gave him the job.

Three months into the Star's newest recruit's tenure, Ffion was reflecting on the wisdom of her choice. The Englishman clearly had a bit of journalistic gumption about him, but he managed to demonstrate on numerous occasions that he could also be, again reflecting back to mid-twentieth-century American authors, *a pretty lazy son of a bitch*.

It was as retribution for two recently missed deadlines that the task with which Adam was charged whilst sat at the office's least favourite desk, was the editor's most favourite form of punishment: "Scan through the minutes of Lancaster Town Council's most recent meeting and find me a juicy news story".

They both knew that the notes from these meetings had about as much juice in them as a squeezed-out lemon. But they also both knew that this was Adam's problem, not Ffion's.

As the editor turned away from him and moved towards her office, she called back over her shoulder, "And don't even think of going to lunch before you can give me 500 words of copy".

Chapter Two

It had been a bad day for Horace Board.

Jermima Billybob, the red hot can't possibly fail to win favourite for the 16:10 race at Brighton, had....failed. Beaten by the nose of Cressex Katie, a twelve to one rank outsider. *Safe Six*, a fancied filly from the Philippines, might just as well have stayed there for the impact she'd had in the 15:10 and *Maythehorsebewithu* had come in next to last in the 15:40. The fact that such a woeful performance was significantly better than *Wearthefoxhat* fared, pulled up a few furlongs from home in the day's final race, provided no comfort.

For some gamblers, you have good days, and you have bad days. Of late, Horace had been managing none of the former and all of the latter. Actually, that's probably stretching the definition of the phrase, *of late*.

The top of the slope had been reached about 18 months ago, shortly after he'd inherited £247,000 and the quarter share of a two-year-old thoroughbred called Beaversmount from a distant Finnish aunt with a *Carry-On* sense of humour. Horace had staked the odd £7k, in her memory, each way on his new horse's first outing after her passing and he would later reflect on that being the beginning of his demise. For the moment *Beaver*, for short, crossed the line at the head of the field at fifteen to two, his hat went in the air and his sense went out the window. Within a fortnight, the £59,500 he'd collected from that win had gone the way of BET365. Within barely three months, the other £240,000 had travelled in a similar direction.

Alas, this apparent nadir marked only the halfway point of Board's descent. One year, to the very day that Aunt Majava had hung up her stirrups for the final time, his premium bonds had been cashed in (proceeds to William Hill); his pension pot crystallised (Ladbrooks); and his four-bedroom detached house overlooking Ryelands Park and within a sand wedge of the River Lune, mortgaged to within a percentage point of its value (Sky Bet).

Now believe it or not, in six months' time, Horace would come to reflect on this current situation with the words, *if only I had stopped there!* Sure, his bank account was barely in single figures, but he owed nothing and he wasn't in anyone's debt. He certainly was at the bottom of a slope, but at least he was still at ground level. Within a matter of weeks, however, Horace had gone subterranean. He was still trying to claw back his losses with a series of complex bets on the gee gees, but now the *Trixes* and *Reverse Yankees* were being funded by several payday loans (29,439% APR, terms and conditions apply). Alas, Hermes continued to look unkindly on him and in no time at all, Horace had little idea where his next penny might come from. Things were bleak. He was feeling a very black Board.

Believe it or not, again, in the months to come he would reflect on this moment with a familiar turn of phrase: *if only I had stopped there!* Because the next step he took wandered into totally uncharted territory.

It may have been Saint Homobonus who once said that the lure of the tailor's cloth is hard to resist for a man with no trousers. So it was for Cllr Board, Chair of Lancaster Council's Finance Committee, as he considered his own absence of assets on the one hand and the Council's reserves fund balance of £807,067 on the other.

He started testing the monetary waters by transferring relatively small amounts from the Council's working account to his own, supported by paperwork that, while bogus, was also plausible and all too easily accepted by whichever unsuspecting colleague he'd conned for a second signature. He was helped by the fact that everyone trusted him; he was very much considered a man above Board.

Horace was careful to ensure his debit amounts never actually appeared on the Council's expenditure sheet. Before each meeting, he would slide sufficient funds from the general reserve to bring the current account back to balance. After a few months, the amounts being slid towards H Board had reached £463,981, while the Council's reserves had plummeted by an identical amount, to £343,086. Ordinarily, one would have thought that such a plunder of Lancaster's rainy-day money would have at least prompted the odd question. However, there were two reasons why the deficit remained undetected and, indeed, appeared not to be causing even so much as a single eyebrow to be raised.

First of all, Horace was juggling the account like crazy, maintaining its balance at the correct level. He achieved this by what is referred to in the financial world as, *kite flying*; taking advantage of the somewhat outmoded way in which the banking system manages non on-line transactions. He started by paying in a cheque from one of his own bank accounts to that of the Council's. The fact that there was little or no money in his account mattered not because before that cheque had cleared and plunged his balance into overdraft (unauthorised), he had credited that account with a cheque from another account he held with a different bank. In total, he had thirty-six personal accounts with a variety of financial institutions at his disposal and within a month there were dozens of cheques from each one of them *doing the rounds*, so to speak. Each cheque deposited would provide a temporary credit balance before the cheque ahead of it on the financial round-a-bout Horace had created was presented for payment. So long as he timed and managed the process properly and did not allow any of the debits or credits to catch up with one another, Horace reckoned it would take the bean counters at the bank a fair few months before the trend was spotted and the ruse rumbled.

He further protected his scheme from detection by every so often bringing the magic round-a-bout of money circulation to a temporary halt. This was achieved by dipping into the Council's deposit funds a little bit further so some real money could be injected into the system. After a week or so, once things had calmed down, he repaid that withdrawal with a personal cheque which in turn restarted the whole process.

The second reason his illegal borrowing had gone undetected was because the cash cow being plundered had remained completely untouched for so many years that no one ever bothered to question it, let alone ask to look tremendously closely at a pucker bank statement. The Finance Chair's comment that, "our reserve funds remain at £807,067" had been rattled off at Council meetings so often that almost everyone could reel off the figure by heart and was more than sufficient for the move to the *next business* to be agreed on the nod. Horace had also become adept at downloading the Council's bank statements online and doctoring out the debits and credits so that, to the casual observer, the deposit account statement looked in total order. Of course, if the cheques and false credits ever stopped doing their rounds, the discrepancy would immediately come to light, but that, Horace hoped, was some time off and a problem for another day.

Of course, with every day that passed, said *another day* was getting ever closer and, while Horace clearly needed to act fast, he had pretty much run out of options and ideas. He hadn't quite reached panic mode, but he was beginning to do whatever is a dozen or so levels above *fret*.

As desperate as Horace felt, however, he always had his eye out for some form of break to resolve his situation and one day, opportunity presented itself in such a way that he would come to wonder whether twelve was to be his new lucky number.

He was among the city's *Great and Good* in St Barnabus Church Hall, where it had become traditional at Christmas for the various public services to put on a show to demonstrate how they were dealing with bad behaviour and petty crime amongst teenagers and young adults. Horace wasn't particularly interested in the topic, but the mayor was desperate to get out of going and he'd drawn the short straw of having to replace him in representing the Council. "Thanks." said His Worship. "You're a star, Board."

The organisers were trying to shepherd everyone from stand to stand, but there was a fair bit of chattering among hoi polloi, which made it difficult for Horace to concentrate on what was going on. First stop appeared to be a group of police officers talking about things they were doing with teenage boys to stop them from getting involved in knife crimes. While at the next table, a couple of teachers seemed to be explaining how they approached getting messages on the harms of smoking across to teenage girls. Horace considered the gender split of these two presentations and could only assume youthful lads were far too busy trying to stab people to take up smoking and young ladies were spending too much of their spare time behind the cycle sheds passing around the Marlborough's to explore the delights of scarring someone for life.

He stood at the back of the pack, distracted by Roy Wood wishing it could be Christmas on a distant radio, again, and his own thoughts - well, 463,981 thoughts to be exact. Suffice to say that he wasn't really paying attention to what was going on. The crowd had been nudged towards the rear of the hall where a social worker was talking about how engaging children in *the arts* could have such a positive effect. Four or five teenagers were scribbling furiously on A0 pads perched precariously on an equal number of easels, all ankle-deep in paint pots, pallets, and torn bits of cartridge paper.

With his mind still absorbed on the problem of how to replenish the Council's coffers, his focus was suddenly nudged away from the budding Leonardos in front of him by something going on outside. A young man, probably in his early 20s, was leaning up against a brick wall covered in graffiti. Judging by the discarded spray cans lying on the floor all around him, it looked as if the *artwork* had been created quite recently. The social worker noticed Horace's attention had been distracted and called out to him, "Do you like the drawing he's done?" Gaining no response, she raised her voice and tried again: "The drawing? Councillor! The drawing, Board?" Giving up, she turned and spoke to the rest of her audience: "....and outside is Paul, our very own Banksy. Or..." the social worker lowered her voice as she was clearly about to relay something in confidence: "....so he tells us. Mind you, he also claims to have met Paul McCartney in the sixties and told him to throw his *scrambled eggs* idea into the recycling and give '*Yesterday*' as the title of his latest song a go. Anyway, just keep an open mind to anything he says to you."

As one, the masses turned to look outside. However, obviously underwhelmed at being directed towards a fantasist's mishmash of the usual tags and squiggles they could see every day on every wall and every tunnel in town, everybody turned pretty much straight back to her. Everyone, that is, except Horace.

The formal presentations over, the Good and the Great shuffled towards the end trestle for the tea and bourbons that had been laid on. Horace, however, veered in the other direction and walked out into the cold air of the courtyard. He watched Paul put a few finishing touches to a picture he recognised as *Girl with a Balloon*, several variants of which he knew *the* Banksy had used in support of social campaigns.

He wandered over to the young man and said, "I say, old boy, what are you working on there? It looks jolly good, whatever it is."

Despite the inoffensive approach Horace had thought he'd manage to adopt in his opening remarks, "Piss off, granddad. Go twirl your moustache somewhere else." was the response he received.

Not quite what he was going for. Horace tried another tack. "So, Paul, is it? You specialise in copying Banksy's do you?"

The lad turned round, glared at him with eyes that seemed to have been sprayed with the darkest black from one of the aerosol cans at his feet. He spat, "Me? Copy him? He's just a *bite*, that's all he is. *Balloon Lass* was a blockbuster I come up with. I first rollered her outside an open factory window in Pooles Warf off Spike Island in Bristol 15 years ago. It was around the time I'd introduced Chas to Princess Di. Anyway, the next thing I know, *Mr Mysterious Banksy* is being lauded all over the planet as the world's greatest street king. There was heaps of interest in who *Secrety Shadowy Man* was, the joker. Some mates put *my* name around – just as a josh – but the press lapped it up and *Covert Guy* did nothing to dissuade the media they'd gotten it all wrong.

Me? Copy him?" he repeated, "He's the Bite. He's the bloody Xerox!"

The unprompted rant rather took Horace aback. The lad was clearly not all there, but that might not prove to be a bad thing. Indeed, he later reflected that at some stage during Paul's bleating and vitriol the basis of an idea, a ridiculous idea, a totally nonsense idea, not only wandered but splashed into his head. It was far from what you could describe as a well-formed plan; a hazy kernel of a thought was somewhat closer to the mark. Nevertheless, Horace had a niggling sense that he might just have stumbled across something here that was worth deeper consideration. And, irrespective of the state of his mind, there was no question about it: the lad could certainly paint.

Paul was turning away and Horace needed to play for some time while trying to structure his thoughts. Thinking perhaps some flattery might throw up something, he asked the lad if he thought his nemesis had done his work proud.

"I don't not know no neminisis. but, I s'pose," he said, pausing for a moment to consider a question he'd never contemplated before: "that despite the fact he sometimes uses some pretty weird backjumps – I once saw him incorporate chalk into a piece of graffiti. Paul looked at Horace's name badge. I mean, come on...chalk, Board - his stuff is rockin'. In fact," he continued, "put his work up against mine and there ain't no one, expert or otherwise, who could tell the difference. I bet you could do a switch, Board. Swap our works around and you'd not tell 'em apart." He then hesitated before adding, "....except from the fact, of course, that his piece would be valued in the millions. I doubt many would even pay something slightly above sod all for a work by Paul Gunningham."

Horace had some serious working out to do. He thanked Paul for his time, told him again how much he loved his work and, taking a note of his mobile number, said "I may just have a little project that might interest you. I'll give you a call. Keep your phone by your side."

He left the church hall, bourbons and tea behind and grabbed a taxi home (putting the fare on the Council's tab). Once inside, he went straight into the living room and plonked himself down in the comfy leather armchair positioned directly beneath the framed picture of a sculpture by Rodin he'd purchased while on a Council exchange visit to Paris. He began to think.

Chapter Three

Within a few hours, Horace thought he'd nailed it. The perfect plan that would brush away his financial woes in one swish of a brush.

He picked up his phone and punched in the number Paul had given him earlier in the day.

The moment his call was answered, Horace launched into schmooze mode. He repeated how much he loved what he'd seen at St Barnabus; what a rum do it was that Banksy seemed to have stolen his thunder, "....AND that he was making money hand over fist from it while you're languishing, preverbally in the gutter, old boy." In fact, Horace exuded every emotion he could think of to gain the street artist's confidence. In the end, he seemed to win Paul over with the story (brilliantly conceived, even if Horace thought so himself) of living next to the neighbours from hell. "They are a nightmare. Absolute perfectionists. Nothing can ever be out of place. If even a mown blade of my grass blows into their garden, all Hades is let loose. They'd go ballistic if any graffiti appeared in view from their bedroom windows. I would love to see their faces on a day they pulled back their curtains to be presented with a clear line of sight direct onto a *Gunningham* in my garden."

Horace let that thought hang in the air. Whether he'd painted an image too enticing to resist, or the boy felt some empathy with the tale, he couldn't tell. But, as his stepfather was fond of saying, *it mattered not,* because, in the end, he persuaded Paul to meet him in Ryelands Park. "I'll WhatsApp you directions. See you shortly." Within moments of Horace ending the call, his message outlining the rendezvous point had winged its way through to Paul's phone:

I'll meet you on the south side of the park, by a bench that sits amidst a small copse of trees along the wall marking the perimeter of the grounds. Look out for two large stone elephants sitting up as if begging on top of the brickwork; they will guide you to the place. The seat is there beneath them. It has a dedication, dated 1964, "In memory of Dennis, who loved this spot. He is much missed".

THE BENCH WAS WELL and truly off what many locals would describe as *the well-beaten track* and hadn't been as straight-forward to find as Paul had expected.

It was getting late in the day; dusk had not quite descended, but the December wind nipping across the open park had reduced the number of people milling around to a minimum. He'd assumed that spotting a couple of elephants in a Lancaster Park might be one of the easier tasks (or tusks, he sniggered to himself) he'd have to carry out today. But, not so much. It took him three or four scans along the top of the brick boundary before he caught sight of a trunk poking out above the trees and bushes. Despite homing in on the landmarks, he still managed to walk past the bench a couple of times – the *copse* was more of what he might have called impenetrable bushes – before finally locating it beneath a box hedge that had been left to go quite ragged. The letters etched on the seat's tarnished plaque were difficult to read at first, but once his eyes had become accustomed to the failing light, Paul was able to make out Dennis's name and satisfy himself that he was in the right place.

Paul sat down, tightened the Shrewsbury Town FC scarf tied around his neck to try and keep out the worst of the wind and gazed around. The very few people who, only moments ago he'd been aware of had disappeared. He turned and reread the dedication, just to double-check he really was in the correct spot. His mind strayed as he pondered the dilapidated state of the bench. He thought it looked like it'd been quite some time since

Dennis really had been much missed. He started creating a mural in his head of Gnasher and Mr Menace searching desperately for a lad in a black and red hooped jersey, when the crack of a stick from behind him banished further comic thoughts from his mind.

He turned his head but didn't immediately recognise the figure now standing over his shoulder. Indeed t took him five or ten seconds before he realised it was Horace who had appeared from the undergrowth.

He bore very little resemblance to the man he'd only met that morning. But then, the figure now moving by his side hadn't had his coat lapels flipped up around his neck against the lowering temperatures, or a cloth trilby pulled down to eyebrow level. If he'd not been expecting to meet Horace here, he wondered if he'd have recognised him at all. But soon Paul regained his composure – and his natural scepticism. "So," he said before the Councillor had the chance to proffer any greetings or pleasantries. "What's the score, Board and what on earth are we doing here in the park? I thought you was aiming to freak out your neighbours with some tags on your garden wall."

Horace unbuttoned the top of his coat and motioned for Paul to follow him through the undergrowth, pushing aside some low hanging branches and navigating around an old dishwasher, washing machine and fridge freezer some ignorant sod had obviously fly tipped. With the bushes and kitchenalia behind them, Paul saw he was facing the wall that he assumed to be no more than a structure marking the perimeter of the park. It stood about fifteen feet high and disappeared out of sight in both directions.

Horace said, "My house is on the other side from here and that's where I want you to do your work, but I thought this would first give you an alternative perspective. Something to practice on. You could perhaps make use of the *blank canvas* on this side of the wall to provoke some inspiration – or even use it as a trial for when you set up in my garden. What I'm thinking......." but his words trailed off as he could see that Paul had stopped listening.

The artist had clearly become transfixed. The long, clean and blank stretch of brickwork must have been as awe-inspiring as any he'd ever seen in his life. "So this is it!" Paul blurted out, not bothering to conceal his excitement. "This is *lit*. Fantastic! And it's exactly the same on the other side? A double canvass. Sic!" He turned to Horace for confirmation that his benefactor was indeed offering him the street artist's chance of a lifetime and he hadn't gotten the wrong end of the stick. Horace, with open arms and slightly hesitantly said, "Enjoy." but then added, "Any ideas?"

Paul clearly had a few thousand in mind, but as if in an instant, they were all funnelled down into one. "Given the Yule time of year," he said, "I'm thinking, Christmas."

Chapter Four

From the cover of the copse, Horace had watched Paul work his way from the banks of the Lune towards his remote section of the park and plonk himself on Dennis's bench. He'd read enough reports on graffiti artists to know that, for the serious ones at least, give them the chance of scrawling on a virgin piece of pristine Council property and they become transfixed. For some, it was almost like being a drug addict; they couldn't help themselves and would do almost anything to feed the habit. Given the chance, Horace would have bet every cent he could have embezzled from the Council that Paul would find the sight of this untouched wall irresistible. Only the absence of any Bookie prepared to make him a market scuppered that idea, but now, judging on Paul's reaction and therefore reluctantly pushing his sure fire bet aside, he could see Master Gunningham was in seventh heaven.

PAUL WAS EXPANDING on his *Christmas* comment. "See the way this section of the wall has been skimmed over with a smooth plaster? The builder must have had a bit of pride about his work because he could have left it at that, all very sweet but pretty boring. Instead, he worked in a bit of definition, marking out what looks to me like one-metre-sized blocks. Can you see them? Here....look at this block, Board. Look. There are," he started counting them out loud for Horace, "one, two, three........ twelve of them, sitting there, all spotless, unspoiled and just waiting for me. Dope!"

Horace nodded enthusiastically. He didn't really have a clue as to what Paul was talking about, but he thought perhaps some vociferous nodding might keep the painter engaged. With Paul getting more and more energised and jabbering as fast and coherently as a Jackson Pollock painting, it seemed to be having the desired effect.

"I could work out some images based on, maybe, twelve...... the disciples. Could I swap them around a bit? Maybe have a *Doubting Judas;* or something around John's old man being called Zebedee – that's always struck me as weird. Was his wife named Florence, or was that the cow? Or no. Not the disciples. Far better than that; The song. The twelve days of Christmas. Yes. That's it. The song. One slab for each day. With a twist. Super sic!"

Slowly, Horace began to see what Paul was proposing – and it sounded like it would fit into his scheme perfectly.

HORACE HAD ARRANGED the meeting in this corner of the park with one key objective.

He'd enticed Paul to come around with the promise of a great space for him to work on and help him get one over on his neighbours. But he couldn't risk being seen with him out in the open, so giving him a tour of his back garden was a nonstarter. Instead, he'd decided on showing him this reverse side of the wall and spouting out some nonsense about how he thought, "....this could offer you an alternative perspective of the final canvas. Something to practice on".

As things were turning out, Horace couldn't imagine the whole scenario going any better. Paul had generated far more than the sufficient enthusiasm he'd hoped for all on his own and was clearly up for the task. He might even get away with him just painting on this side of the wall and avoid the complications of working in his garden at all. And the copse, trench coat, hat and twilight must surely have done their job of preventing anyone from recognising him, not that he could recall seeing any passersby who might have witnessed their meeting.

Yes, all elements of *phase one* had come together nicely and although he felt more than justified in giving himself a gold star, he was conscious that this change in plan did raise a couple of significant issues. Horace pushed one of those aside for the moment but made a mental note that he would have to sort that out later. More pressing would be finding a way of restricting the size of the artwork. Whatever creative trip Paul embarked on, Horace needed to ensure it didn't cross beyond the boundaries of the brickwork he owned. Limiting Paul's work in his garden would have been easy: the lateral fences and bushes dividing his property from his neighbours' made it obvious what section of the wall was his and what was not. But from where they currently stood in the park, the brickwork just seemed to stretch on for miles.

However, as he looked a little more closely at the defining dozen sections of plaster Paul was now raving over, he could see that all twelve were well and truly within his boundary.

He'd bought the house off plan before it was built and had, as such, been afforded some ability by the developer to request a few personal touches be included in the work. There weren't really many changes Horace wanted. He asked for the double oven to be swapped to a single and a microwave; for the doors of the built-in 'fridge and washing machine to open the other way "so us southpaws can use them more easily"; and that a fitted loft ladder be installed. He was all but ready to give his final signoff when he recalled the two huge stone elephants his grandfather had brought back from India following its independence from the British. Apparently, for decades they had stood proudly, each on top of a magnificent wall either side of the gate and marking the entrance to the ambassador's residence in Tamil Nadu where he had worked as Assistant Attaché up to 1947. Upon receiving notification he was to be recalled to the Foreign Office in London, Grandpa Board, who had long admired what locals regarded as great statues of power and strength thought, "I'm 'aving those".

Horace had lost count of the number of times he'd heard his grandfather's *go to* story as to how they came to be in his possession. How he and Rushdawa, his *punkhawallah,* had crept out under the cover of darkness on the night before his ship home was due to sail and began unscrewing the stone beasts from their brass mounts. "I was determined to take them home with me, come what may." he confided to his grandson. "I were a bit worried when we lost our grip and both mammoths crashed to the ground, making a sound that would have woken Ghandi himself. But the security guards must have had a skinful 'cause they didn't stir an inch. We simply loaded the booty onto a couple of wheelbarrows, crudely covered them with tarpaulins and walked the rozzers, as stone faced as the figures we were sneaking away with. Right past and under their snoozin' noses."

Of course, sometimes, well, many times, actually the yarn would be embellished. On occasions grandpa claimed there were eight uniformed officers on duty. Sometimes the figure was twenty; it all depended on how many Bombay Sapphires and tonics he'd had by the time his latest rendition of the tale started. But irrespective of the true number of less than watchful eyes his ancestor and his accomplice had thwarted, by the time the sun had risen the following morning on the countless Dravidian-style Hindu temples in this southern Indian state, the two enormous sculptures had been boxed up in a couple of crates and shipped home to Blighty, concealed in plain sight alongside the four steamer trunks containing his personal belongings.

Horace had literally stumbled across the dubiously purloined mementoes many moons later, while clearing out his late father's property. He had managed to machete his way through to the back of his dad's overly cluttered shed when he stubbed his toe against something sharp. Despite his pain, he realised he'd come across the mementos from Madras and could only assume they had lain here, untouched and forgotten, since being passed down from his grandfather. But he, in turn, had done little more than simply relocate them to the rear of his own outhouse, where they were again forgotten.

Until then.

The imminent move to his new home demanded another clear out be undertaken and resulted in the Indian keepsakes resurfacing.

Standing upright on two feet and with their trunks stretching proudly above their heads, they looked as if they'd been frozen in time halfway through a circus act. Each elephant was about the size of the average, obese American, although both would have come in at two or three times that country's mean weight. What was not in the least bit surprising was that there had been no place for them in Horace's one-up, half-down flat in the town. However, he thought, on the corners of the garden wall that would be built at the foot of his new property to shield him off from the dog walkers in Ryelands Park, they would be perfect. The builder, in a desperate effort to get this particular commission signed off (and this pernickety client off his back), agreed to fix the beasts on the wall, although he was less than sure as to just how secure he could make them. "These damn things weigh a ton." he explained, "And they're completely the wrong shape to sit steadfastly on the wall." In the end, the builder cemented them as best he could. His parting shot was that they'd stay put in a high wind, but he wouldn't plan on standing anywhere below them if a tornado came along.

Comfortable in the fact that Lancaster wasn't overly affected by cyclones or twisters, Horace was just pleased to have his grandfather's plunder back out in the open and in plain sight. However, when all is said and done, these were still only a couple of lumps of decorative stone on a wall at the foot of his garden. It wasn't long before they returned to being largely forgotten.

Until now.

The twelve slabs Paul was focusing on sat neatly beneath and within the confines of the brace of beasts that marked the edges of Chez Board.

"Well, I'm glad you like it." said Horace. "Just use it to get the paint juices flowing with your Christmas design here first – then you can attack the other side with some real gusto."

Paul was glazing over and seemed more than enthused by the free range he was being given. Horace looked on and thought his plan – and this hasty revision - was coming together nicely. He still needed to give a coat of weighing up to the other problem that working on this side of the wall would mean, but for the moment, that had to take a back seat. He first needed to make sure Paul was committed to the task and fix the time and date he'd actually make a start.

Chapter Five

"It's best if I do things at night." Paul said. "That ain't because it makes avoiding being spotted or nabbed a little easier – although it does - but at night I seem to get a better feel for the art. I've cobbled together a blingin' contraption that fits under my cap and works a bit like a miner's lamp. The way the light it throws combines with the spray from the aerosol just seems to lead me on and on to bigger and better stuff. It's incredible. Really sic!"

"Well, don't get here too early", Horace instructed. "Leave it 'till after the pubs have turned out and the addicts who kip out in the park have had a chance to get well and truly off their heads. How long do you think you will need to complete your Christmas homage?" Paul said that if he got here around midnight, he should be done by three in the morning.

Horace asked about all the paints and sprays. "I imagine it's tempting providence to just walk about with them bold as brass. What happens if the odd nosey copper....gets nosey?"

Paul explained that that can be a problem, particularly if you're caught with all the gear walking across some wide-open spaces at night. Being nabbed in the wee small hours in possession of twelve cans of spray paint, some stencils and an array of brushes can be a difficult situation to talk one's way out of. "But it's a lot less risky when the sun's up." he explained. "Police have all but given up on random *stop and search* during the day – especially for those with my colouring. No, once I've identified a site, I try to get my equipment in place ahead of time. I've got it all sorted and down to a fine art. I pack away my sprays and brushes into a blue and amber rucksack. Everyone assumes it's football related; it is, but then again," he winked at Horace, "it ain't, if you know what I mean. Then there's a special bag that clips onto the bottom that contains me stairs." Horace wasn't at all sure what he meant by that, but let it pass. Paul was in full flow.

"I like to find a neat place, nearby to the canvas, where I can hide the lot away in advance while it's still light. That way everything I need is ready and waiting for me to turn up and I can get down to work immediately. If anyone stops me on the way to the job, I've got nothing with me. I'm just a guy out for a walk in the moonlight."

Horace did a 360-degree sweep of the area and said, "You could perhaps leave your bags here behind Dennis's bench. No one is likely to stumble across anything there, are they?"

Paul agreed and said he'd make sure everything was in place over the next couple of days. "In less than forty-eight hours you are going to have one heck of a rough copy ready for your approval. If you like what you see, it will be a cinch to redo it on your side of the wall, brother Board. And I guarantee it will stun your neighbours. They'll be as speechless as Olga Korbut was when I scored a ten on the beam the week before she won the Olympics. Horace, when they see what I'm going to do, they'll go absolutely Christmas crackers!"

Chapter Six

The morning after his clandestine meeting with Paul, and in order to get everything in place for the following evening's event, Horace set to work making five phone calls. The first of which was to his neighbour at number 3, Primary Avenue.

"Jules. Sorry to ring so early, but I wanted to catch you before you went to work. I've got a delivery coming sometime today or tomorrow that needs to be signed for, but I'm on call for Council business. Sod's law it'll arrive when I'm out. I don't suppose you're going to be home at all to be able to take this in for me?"

Jules apologised that she wouldn't be able to help; she was about to drive to Whitby for the launch of a new book called *The Huntrodds Coincidences* by her latest protégé and wouldn't be back before the weekend.

The response to Horace's identical enquiry to Stef at number 7 provided a similar outcome. "We're just off to our daughter's in Devon to look after the grandkids; we'll be away until Saturday. They're into canoeing of all things, so we're taking them out to mess about on the River Dart, Board. Sorry."

Little did either neighbour know, but their absences suited the resident, sandwiched between them at number 5, perfectly.

The third call was the one about which he was most nervous, although as things turned out, there was to be no cause for concern. He was put straight through to the duty sergeant at Lancaster's police station (one of the benefits of being able to let slip your "Councillor" title) and immediately started bumbling through a slightly incoherent, albeit very well-rehearsed, explanation as to why he was phoning.

"I'm probably being very silly, so please don't go to any great lengths, but there's been someone hanging around in the Avenue lately. I'm not sure I've seen them before and he just looks a little suspicious, not that I can quite put my finger on it but, with my neighbours both being away at the moment and all........."

Sargent Greig took the opportunity of the break in Horace's monologue to interject. "Councillor Board. You shouldn't feel at all embarrassed or hesitant contacting us about this sort of thing. If you are ever worried in any way at all, you should always call the station. That's exactly what I'm here for."

Sargent Greig sighed, hopefully not so loud that Horace could hear and reflected, not for the first time during such a call, that, if truth be told, he did *not* think this was exactly the sort of thing he was there for at all. It certainly wasn't the sort of incident that had prompted him to join the force in the first place.

Tony Greig had left his native Australia as a teenager nearly forty years ago, mainly in search of a better life but also because he was fed up with the endless jibes he received over sharing his name with the then England cricket captain. He'd boarded a boat bound, ultimately, for Britain, but with the intention of jumping ship once it reached the Panama Canal. However, midway between Hobart and Hawaii, Tony became involved with a couple of professional fraudsters in such a way that changed both his Panama plan and his life.

The first time he saw them was in the Purser's Bar shortly after setting sail. They were deep in conversation with a middle-aged and, considering the cool temperatures on board, heavily overdressed lady. There was a jug of Castlemaine XXXX and what looked like a small sherry on the table between them, although the drinks had barely been touched. While there was nothing particularly unusual about this whole scenario that might have captured Tony's attention, his ears did prick up when he overheard them make mention of a mining settlement called *Cue*. Now Cue was not a place many people had ever heard of. And those who had would rarely bother speaking about it. Tony Greig, however, who had grown up in this small, non-descript town in the mid-west of Western Australia, was one of the few. On the day, some fifty years ago, when his parents bundled him and his sister into the family Holden and left its confines for the more civilised southeast corner of the continent, the population plummeted by over two and a half percent. To 153. It was now a distant part of Tony's life, but a part with fond memories nevertheless and to hear its mention automatically attracted his interest.

The trio showed no indication of being aware that a snotty teenager was even in the room, so they didn't seem particularly guarded about what they were saying. As a result, however, it became all too apparent – particularly for someone familiar with this neck of WA – that something slightly fishy was going on.

The talk was of the huge opportunities to be had by investing in the exotic-sounding *Big Bell*, *Comet* and *Day Dawn* mining centres. The two men spoke with wide eyes and huge gestures. Maps and papers were being produced and laid out before the heavily coated Sherry woman to gaze down on. "Look at the projection figures for the amount of gold throughout this region of Australia. In some places it's all but just lying there on the ground with barely even the need to pick up a pick to prise the yellow mineral from the rock."

Now, as a former native of this place, Tony knew two things about what he had just overheard. Firstly, the spiel was accurate. The initial estimates of the gold value in these mines were in the millions and millions of dollars. However, the second fact was that those estimates were made in the late 1800s. By the time Dr and Mr G had relocated their family to set up a health clinic in Warrnambool, Victoria, the gold cupboard in Cue was well and truly bare. "There ain't no more gold left in them there mines." was an oft heard quote by the locals referencing a shortage of any kind. Tony knew that anyone saying anything different was unlikely to be up to any good. He also knew that, if either of his parents had been here, one or other of them would have told him not to sit idly by.

The first official he found to speak with about his concerns was the barman, who gave him short shrift and told him to bugger off. He received similar suggestions from the Third Engineer and Second Mate. It wasn't until he'd managed to collar the Medical Purser, whose mother was born in Warrnambool and so took a modest shine to the lad, that he managed to get someone to listen.

With the consent of the captain, a covert operation was put in place and, to cut a long story short, the two men who had been preying on the single [and wealthy] female passengers of this shipping company for some time by trying to scam them out of their cash with bogus Australian mining share certificates were caught.

Tony Greig's part in the fraudsters' capture did not go unrecognised and he was well rewarded by the grateful shipping line. He stayed on board, upgraded to First – until Southampton where he was given a job in the security arm of the firm. Five years later, and with a well-embedded sense of duty and doing the right thing, he left the south coast with glowing references to take up a position in Lancashire's police constabulary. To no one's surprise, least of all his, he achieved promotion within four years.

Anyway, suffice to say that, with his elbows on the counter and staring down the hearing end of the receiver, Sargent Greig did not feel this sort of middle-class paranoia was anywhere close to the reason he was either so committed to public service or donned a uniform every day at all. However, deciding that expressing such sentiments to a local Council official might not be the best way to make Inspector any time soon, he continued his line of appeasement. "I'm sure, as you suspect, there's a perfectly reasonable explanation [he really doubted Horace suspected any such thing], but I'll get a police car to drive by the next time one is in the area [perhaps you'd like me to pull someone away from a murder enquiry]. Maybe a little bit of visible policing will do the trick." [or at least get you off my back for a few hours].

Horace thanked the duty officer profusely. "It probably is nothing at all, so please don't do anything out of the ordinary, but you've certainly put my mind at rest, so thank you for that."

As he returned the handset to its cradle, Horace felt that couldn't possibly have gone any better. There will be a formal log of his call, but the last thing he wanted was a brigade of police calling over the place—at least, not just yet, anyway........

Call number four was to Ira Taken, Head of Council's Parks and Community Spaces department.

The moment Ira answered the phone, Horace swept in with the same little joke he used at the start of every conversation he had ever had with this official. "Ah, Miss Taken, if I'm not mistaken."

Ira stifled a sigh.

"I'd appreciate a bit of advice please." Horace continued.

Although born in the central Ukrainian city of Poltava, Ira had spent most of her adult life in England and prided herself on understanding virtually every facet of her adopted country's culture as well as the next woman. The one area that she just couldn't get to grips with however, was the propensity of the English to pun at any opportunity. It just isn't an aspect of humour that has travelled successfully to her native homeland. There is an old Ukrainian saying, *Nemaye dymu bez vohnyu*. It doesn't translate well into English, but in essence it means: there should be punishment where a pun is meant. Alas, this eastern European warning has been equally unsuccessful in travelling the other way, so it remains largely ignored on this side of the channel – particularly, she lamented, in Lancaster.

Ira had, of course, heard the line many times before. Particularly from Councillor Board. Her predecessor, Tamara Osnovnikh had suffered "Ah, I see it's Tamara.....or is it today?" from him every month for five years before moving on. Her parting gift to Ira was the suggestion that, any time she encountered the punning Councillor, just look back impassively while picturing a group of *povia*, ladies of the night, running a 4 x 100 metre relay. From that moment on, Ira followed this advice whenever and however Horace spoke with her. Even at the end of the phone, she still went through the process of conjuring up her usual image of garishly dressed women on the starting line in Beijing's Birds Nest stadium. With that picture firmly embedded in her mind and staring blankly at the wall in front of her, she asked the Councillor what she could do for him.

Horace explained that a few local ruffians had sprayed paint on the other side of his garden wall and wondered, given that it faced out onto the park and that they'd clearly grafittised his property while standing on Council property, whether the Council's Park's department might pay to have it removed.

Ira was used to people – usually the general public but, alas all too often Council officials as well – trying things on in this way, so was well practiced in her response. "I'm afraid not, Councillor. All aspects of the wall, be they the coping stones on the top, or the brickwork you can't see from your garden, are the owner's responsibility."

There was a short pause at the end of the line before Horace said, "So this has absolutely nothing whatsoever to do with the Parks department?"

Ira confirmed to him that any necessary repair, irrespective of how it was caused, does indeed have nothing at all to do with the Council. "The wall – and everything on or about it - is yours to repair and manage as you see fit. The Council has no interest in it whatsoever."

That piece of advice prompted nothing bar a further pause from Horace and gave Ira hope that she had successfully brought the matter to a close. She finished the call by advising the Councillor that, in accordance with Council Regulation 72, para 4, sub section 18(iv) – dealing with financial requests for Council funds from elected officials - she was required to report this conversation to the Council Secretary for him to record it in the minutes of the next Town Council meeting.

Which is exactly what Horace had hoped she would do.

Horace's final call was to his "go-to" person in the Council's procurement team, Joanne Lead. A year or more ago, while undertaking his chair of finance duties a little more seriously than normal, he had uncovered a few modest discrepancies that Joanne had inadvertently signed off on. Thinking that some future leverage in this department might come in handy, he had convinced her that, while these were sackable, if not imprisonable offences, he had a kind heart and would do his best to overlook them and keep her out of trouble. From that moment on, Horace had an inside ally, always ready to help whenever he called.

Once through to Procurement, he opened with his usual line to Joanne. "Ah. Miss Lead. I'm not sure you can help me. I need someone I can rely on."

Joanne Lead laughed as heartily as Ira Taken.

Horace ploughed on, oblivious to any possible slight and told her the Council was thinking of insuring some very large or big-ticket items and he wanted some advice on who we should, but equally important should not, approach.

The *plan*, for want of a better word, that had shot into Horace's mind while talking with Paul in the outside space behind the church hall was, to say the least, sparsely formed. Indeed, it was little more than a couple of loose ideas. (1) Somehow convince this chap to paint a copycat Banksy looking mural on his wall; and (2) somehow sell it to repay the money he owed the Council.

He had initially convinced himself that the painting's lack of authenticity would matter not a jot. Surely these things were done on a buyer beware" basis? But that afternoon, while sitting beneath the gaze of *Le Penseur*, the more he'd thought about it, the less convinced of that he became. After all, he reasoned with himself: these things were bound to work both ways: if there was a Buyer Beware clause, it was almost certain that there would've been a Term or Condition a little way further down the sale's contract that said, "Vender, you'd better watch out too!" And any come backs from an unsatisfied or unconvinced purchaser would suit neither his perilous financial position nor elaborate scheme.

No. He needed to be able to come out of this deal with no repercussions, and selling the "Banksy" risked someone, somehow finding out that the 'Banksy' they'd bought weren't no Banksy at all. The evidence would need to be destroyed, which is where the idea of getting it insured came to him.

Horace had needed to work fast. In a day or so, Paul would be scribbling and spraying away, creating his masterpiece. If he could get said masterpiece insured - and then somehow make it disappear – he could claim the insurance money without the risk of there being any comebacks.

It was therefore the insurance companies to avoid that Horace was most interested in hearing about from Joanne. And her comments on a firm called, Gill, Wills, James, Farr & Andrews caught his attention.

Miss Lead warned Horace that the firm had a new head of fine arts who is really keen to make an impression. "I think her name is Cumaway or Dunaway or something. Anyway, she's under serious pressure to toss caution to the wind and take on business at the riskier end of the market. Indeed," Joanne continued, "some of my contacts in the insurance world have warned me she's just cutting corners and not doing due diligence in the way she should. They've already had a few losses from some questionable assets she's covered and if they continue in that vein, I worry they might not be around much longer. I think, out of all the firms in the market, you should avoid this one like the plague."

He scribbled down the details of Gill, Wills, James, Farr & Andrews on a piece of paper by his phone: "Just to make absolutely sure I don't contact them by mistake, Miss Lead." and placed it neatly in one of the folds of his wallet.

Horace smiled to himself as he put down the phone. He had pretty much heard all he'd needed to hear. Now, he just had to wait for the early morning hubbub, such as it was in The Avenue, to die down. He had some things to do and wanted to do them with as few people about as possible.

Chapter Seven

Two nights later and Horace couldn't sleep, though this was due more to anticipation than fear.

The room at the back of his large, three-story Victorian house looked out directly over the top of the wall at the end of his garden and into the park. He mainly used it as a sort of den, although tonight it was going to be his crow's nest. He slid a chair over by the window, put his elbows on the sill, his chin in his hands and peered out into the dark night.

That was at seven forty-five.

By seven fifty, he was bored. And his elbows hurt. He got up and repositioned the TV so he could remain watchful at his post yet be able to pay equal attention to whatever was being broadcast.

Within five minutes he'd scrolled through the channels and, deciding there was nothing on, did what he always did in such circumstances and settled down to re-binge watch one of his favourite programmes, *The Dectectorists*.

He'd just reached the early stages of episode three, series two, where Russell and Hugh embark on their mission to recover the mayor's chain of office from a car park in Barnfather Woods, when something outside caught his attention.

He turned away from the developments in Danebury and stared out over his garden, narrowing his eyes, willing them to adjust to the lack of light. He had almost come to the disappointing conclusion it must have been the movement of a squirrel or fox that had attracted him, but then what was unmistakably the flicker of a torch caused his heart to jump.

At last, he thought. Paul had arrived.

Horace felt he could now relax a fraction and returned to his armchair and television. Over the next couple of hours, Horace caught glimpses of the beam from the flashlight bobbing up and down and side to side. Paul was clearly hard at work.

Chapter Eight

Paul had intended to wait until he was sitting on Dennis's bench and well under cover of the trees and bushes before switching on his little light contraption, but despite having been here barely twelve hours earlier secreting away the tools of his trade, the absence of any light in this section of the park had made that impossible. He'd already spent ten minutes groping around for *The Menace's* seat in the pitch black before realising he was actually groping around in completely the wrong copse. Anyway, with a flick of the switch by the peak of his cap, the strong beam that flooded the immediate area enabled him to relocate to the correct spot and consider his next move.

Kneeling on the bench, with his back to the park, he started to mentally position the shapes and colours he'd been tossing over in his mind for the past couple of days onto the dozen neat squares on the wall in front of him. Ever since coming up with the idea, he'd had the words to *The 12 Days of Christmas* spinning around in head non-stop. If nothing else, that helped him to become convinced – even if he hadn't been before – that the last things he'd want to give or, come to that, receive were some ducks, milkmaids or pipe players! He considered making a case for accepting a quinary of auric metal hoops but dismissed that as being a sell-out. It would have to be one in/twelve in and settling on sketches as unimaginative as, say, ten members from the UK's upper chamber jigging about was not a price he thought worth paying. Instead, he'd decided to create more of a homage or reference to each verse in the song rather than a literal depiction.

Grabbing hold of the bag of tricks he'd left underneath Dennis, he pulled out a special glitter paint he'd purchased especially for the occasion. Remembering the constant words of Miss Potter, his first primary school teacher and making sure not to go over the edges, he neatly sprayed its contents over all twelve squares, giving him a beautiful yet delicate background on which to work.

From the bag clipped onto the ruck sack, he pulled out his collapsible step ladder. It was an old and battered paint smeared metal contraption that concertinaed down to almost nothing. While this was the sort of thing many people might just have thrown on a skip without a moment's thought, Paul would not be without it for the world. Given the high spaces and areas he'd often had to reach, this piece of equipment was just as important to him as his paints and brushes.

Springing it open and into action, the penultimate rung brought him perfectly level with the top of the wall such that he could see over and into Horace's garden. There was a light on in an upstairs' bedroom, but it was too far up to cast any meaningful rays to ground level. Returning to the task and with a black spray can in hand, he whooshed the number **12** neatly and subtly in the bottom right-hand corner of the top right-hand square. He'd shaped the number in the style of his favourite **Gill sans ultra-bold** font (chosen out of respect to his first ever love, a lass named Gillian who was gentle and the very opposite of brazen) that he always used for numbers.

Selecting a silver-based paint, he drew twelve star style finger-rings, each with five points and, despite the limited area he had to work with, made sure all were suitably garish and sparkly. The rings were of various sizes and at different angles within the confines of the block and through each one was looped a single, identical golden hoop.

Jumping off the ladder but not stopping even for a moment to admire or assess the result of this first effort, he moved diagonally across to the bottom left hand corner square. A single swoosh had the necessary number **1** in place and within a moment he was using only the black paint, in different thicknesses and shades, to sketch a busker, complete with a harmonica looped around his neck, symbols tied to his knees and a huge base drum strapped to his back. The only glint of colour he permitted involved two dabs of *azure blue* for the street entertainer's eyes. This was one of Paul's more complex compositions and it had taken him just over a half an hour to complete.

Conscious he had to get a shift on he sidled two blocks along, quickly dobbed a **3** in its corner and set to work on a modest canine scene. Within the wag of a tail he was putting the finishing touches to the noses of a prial of white poodles, sitting up on their hind legs in front of the Eiffel Tower and staring out from the canvass. Their mouths were open, their tongues were lopping and Paul was done. Ready to move on.

Switching up a row, he drew a **5** in the box above the busker and, using a selection of white and grey pastilles drew an ice cream cone, an igloo, a *Carlsberg lager tin* and a refrigerator, with a scene of lightly falling snow in the foreground.

By now, Paul had got into a sort of rhythm and within a quarter of an hour he had a pair of trainers marked with the brand, *YEEZY BOOST 350* safely inside box number **2** to the left of the dogs, and eleven bags of crisps painted in square **11** on the top row beside the rings.

Six blocks down, six to go. Paul lowered his head and shone the torch onto his wrist; it was half past one. Blimey, he thought. How time flies when you're having fun.

The following hour was a bit of a blur. Not only with regards to the frantic spraying and brushing that was taking place, but also in Paul's head as he tried to remember how he'd planned each separate piece to look – and even how he might improve on that now he was in situ.

Despite their complexities, the middle two blocks in the middle row were completed in double quick time. Box **6** showed half a dozen East End hoodlums attacking some poor defenceless wretch on the ground. Paul had wanted the viewer to have the impression they were watching the Kray brothers and four of their henchmen on a *typical* night out. He only hoped popping a crude pub-sign saying *The Blind Beggar* in the top corner wouldn't be over egging the pudding. This horrific sight was balanced by the hopefully more tranquil scene in Box **7** of a septet of men treading water in the river beneath the *Morfa bridge*, each with the Welsh emblem adorned on their scull-caps.

The brace of blank boxes on the top line were a tad trickier than the previous pair and so took a tad longer to complete. Having painted the **9** in its place, rather than setting straight to work he lent over to the adjacent square and drew in the **10**. It was as if he didn't quite know how either picture was going to turn out and was stalling for time. In the end however he was able to look back on these two sections with a degree of pride. The rustic feel of his scene involving nine ladybugs, each delicately linked with her partner by their wing tips and circling a campfire nearly brought a tear to his eye; while the comedic effect of ten members of the Marylebone Cricket Club, with stereotypically white handlebar moustaches, bouncing on a trampoline wearing nothing but their iconic red and yellow stripped ties drawn large enough to cover all aspects of their modesty, bought a satisfied grin to his face. They'd taken longer to do than he'd planned, but felt the time spent was certainly worth it.

By contrast, box number **4** in the bottom right hand corner was crafted, coloured and completed within a nano. Admittedly, a quartet of *Tweety-Pies* each with a megaphone held up to their lips, fell some way short of the esoteric vibe Paul had been trying to go with, but hey. What the heck. The scrawny yellow cartoon characters reminded him of his youth (maybe even, Miss Potter?) and made him smile. Surely critics would permit him this one simple indulgence.

And anyway, he still had one last square to complete - although at that moment, he had not the feintest idea what form this final piece of the jigsaw should take.

Deciding the only way forward was to stop trying to overthink things, he neatly drew an **8** in the appropriate spot of the blank square at the end of the middle row and prayed for some inspiration. Well, St Luke must have been having a quiet night in with nothing better to do because within moments an idea had flashed straight to Paul's brush tips. On the left half of the block he drew eight pairs of horizontal parallel lines, while on the right-hand side he sketched an identical number of brown cows facing them.

It was not perhaps the best of the twelve days of Christmas he'd now completed, but at least he'd returned to esoteric mode. Every work of art should have varying degrees of subtlety and enigma – and day 8 would just have to be out there in left field.

Chapter Nine

Horace's original plan had been to orchestrate things such that the police would catch Paul red-handed with a bag of his neighbours' stolen goods while grafittising in his own back garden. Of course, having decided to stay with and use Paul's "dummy run" on the park side of his wall he'd had to rework that.

The morning after meeting Paul by the bench therefore, and as soon as he had established his neighbours' houses would be vacant, Horace had set about the riskiest part of his revised scheme.

The three adjacent neighbours of Primary Avenue had long left spare copies of their door keys with each other to cover "eventualities". They even had a *WhatsApp* group labelled, The Three Primary Colours, through which each could call to the other for the odd cup of sugar or to take receipt of any unexpected parcels. The relationship between the prial of neighbours was close and strong. Horace popping in to The Soskett's to water their plants or putting a bottle of milk the local delivery woman had left on Ellie Jeddow's front step into her fridge, were such commonplace activities they wouldn't cause a single curtain across the street to twitch. And so, when Horace crossed the thresholds of 3 and 7 the day Paul Gunningham was due to start work, but while Mr and Mrs Soskett were in Surrey and Ms Jeddow somewhere up the northeast coast of England, there was not so much as quiver of lace anywhere in the road.

On this day however, had a Mr or Mrs Parker been taking less of a casual approach to their Neighbourhood Watch duties, they might have wondered if indeed something untoward was occurring in their little nook of tranquil paradise. For example, was that sound they'd just heard some panes of glass being smashed? And why had their local Councillor slipped into his neighbours' houses carrying what appeared to be an empty brown leather bag, but that looked more than full to bulging by the time he'd returned to his base at Number 5?

Horace had done his best to muffle the noise that putting his claw hammer through his two neighbours' back door windows would inevitably make by wrapping it in a duster and putting down some strategically placed mats. (He'd also remembered to avoid the rookie mistake made by many a dopey criminal in The Sweeny or almost any other crime TV drama you could name, of not smashing the glass from inside the house. This had to look like an outside job).

The leather bag, once back at number 5 and resting on his dining table, contained a number of small items he'd purloined that he hoped would be viewed as the sort of pieces any acclaimed burglar would be likely to snaffle. Stuff that would be easy to fence, as he thought D.I. Regan might phrase it: silver picture frames, bronze statues, any cash that was lying around and the odd bit of jewellery. Nothing overly large, he had to be able to carry it himself after all, nor ridiculously valuable. He needed to attract the local police's interest but didn't want to create some huge criminal case that might push things over the top and bring in Interpol!

When circumstances dictated that the *Banksy* would be located on the park side of his wall, it was obvious that this bag of incriminating evidence would need to be secreted nearby.

This had caused Horace some concern on two counts: first of all, the bag would not be in his direct sight and indeed would be out in the open where some nosey kid or the odd *ne're do well* looking for a sheltered place to pop her or his head down for the night might stumble across it. Secondly, if he did get lucky and the swag remained undiscovered by the local riff raff before His Majesty's finest were eventually on the scene, would they manage to stumble over it themselves without any of the helpful nudges he'd have been able to give from his own garden?

It was around mid-afternoon that, from the top bedroom in his house, Horace had seen Paul toting the blue and amber ruck sack he guessed was full of brushes and paints, cross the park heading for Dennis's bench. He reappeared a few moments later, sans sack, and started making his way back into town. Once Paul was well and truly out of sight, Horace hoisted the swag bag over his shoulder and went outside through the rear patio doors and down towards an old wooden work bench at the foot of his garden. Clambering up onto its top, he was just able to see over the wall and into the park. Confident no one else was hanging around, he threw the bag, a shovel he'd collected en route, and, a little less recklessly, himself over the wall. He crouched down into the bushes by the bench below and surveyed the scene. He soon found the spot where Paul had hidden his paints and, selecting an area just a few yards away, dug a hole big enough to conceal half the bag from a casual passer-by, but not so deep that it would be missed by anyone consciously looking for something.

It was hard to completely satisfy himself as to just how the bag should be positioned, but in the end, deciding he'd done as best as he could do, scrambled out of the copse and began making his way back home, hoping that for once, luck would come over to his side.

Chapter Ten

By a quarter past two, Jonny Flynn's theme tune was signalling the end of the second episode in the sitcom's third series and Horace decided the time to set the next stage of his plan into motion had arrived.

He picked up his phone and redialled a number he'd rung the day before. It was answered almost immediately: "Lancaster police, good evening. Duty Sargent Greig speaking: How can I help?"

Horace began speaking quite quickly, yet quietly and with what he hoped might come across as a slight degree of panic. "Ah, Sargent Greig. Cllr Board here. We spoke yesterday about some unusual activity on Primary Avenue? Well, a few moments ago I heard the sound of a window smashing next door and I've just seen someone in my back garden clambering over my wall and into the park."

The police officer considered for a moment whether this was still all a complete waste of [his] time and [the taxpayer's] money but felt he couldn't risk fobbing the caller off a second time. So simply and with authority, he said, "Leave it with me, Councillor. I'll send someone around to have a look. And don't you worry: if we find anyone, their feet won't touch the floor, Board."

Horace replaced his receiver, went out of the patio doors and crept down to the foot of his garden. As quietly as possible, he clambered up onto the old wooden workbench and popped his head above the top of the wall. He craned his neck just far enough to be able to see the top of Paul's head, silhouetted by the light from his lamp, a few feet below him. Now all he had to do was wait.

Chapter Eleven

Taking as many paces back from the wall as he could without falling over the discarded dishwasher directly in his line, Paul looked up to admire his work. While some of the blocks were perhaps better than others, he was still fairly pleased with the overall effect.

He considered his Lords and Ladies were all quite quirky; loved the subtlety of the rings, the swimmers and the crisp packets; gave himself several pats on the back for the obtuseness of the East End gangsters, the dogs, the icy items and the branded footwear; and was proud as punch at having included the reference to a 1970's busker's greatest hit, with just a couple of dabs of blue. The Tweety-pies were growing on him and he was even coming to accept that few people outside of France were likely to untangle the workings of the eighth block - at least, not first time.

All in all, he thought. I've managed a dozen pretty good days of Christmas.

He checked his watch. It was half past two. Precisely.

Suddenly, the area around him was bathed in light. He turned and found himself staring into the lenses of a couple of torches, which were moving steadily towards him from either side of the bench. "Police! Freeze! Drop whatever you're holding and put your hands in the air where I can see them." was the shout that came from behind one of the lights. That was quickly followed by "What you doin' here?" from behind the other.

Paul's first reaction, probably quite understandably, was to take heed of the first instruction and so he promptly froze. However, before he had a chance to comply with commands numbered two and three, a voice from above him yelled, "That's him. That's the chappie I saw hanging around a couple of days ago. I'm sure of it. Get him, arrest him; don't let him get away."

Paul looked up, but it was so dark he could only see the outline of the figure who seemed intent on trying to direct police manoeuvres in his general direction. However, all was made clear a second or so later when one of the officers swooshed his torchlight towards the shouting voice, revealing

Councillor Horace Board's head ranting down on the three of them. If the arrival of two of His Majesty's finest in the copse a few moments previously had come as a bit of shock, seeing Horace screaming down at him had him totally confused. "Oi, Board. It's me, Paul Gunningham. What's going on? Tell these geezers who I am."

The policeman, who until now had kept his beam pointing directly at Paul, moved it to join his colleague's light, further illuminating Horace. He called out, "Councillor Board, is that you up there? Do you know this man?"

Horace started shrieking that he'd never seen him before in his entire life, other than perhaps when he was sure it was him he'd clocked vaulting over his neighbour's garden wall yesterday or the day before. "I think he was carrying a brown bag of some description, Constable." he said.

Paul was finding this all very difficult to take in. The owner of the voice above, with whom he had thought he was in cahoots, was now suggesting to the officers that they clap him in irons and throw away the key. Paul was beginning to get the feeling that this didn't have the air of something that was going to turn out well. But then, realising that with both torches pointing over the top of his head and that he was now standing in total darkness, thought this might be an extremely good time to try and get the hell out of there. Turning away from the wall, he started to make for the open park. However, he had barely managed two strides before his foot became caught in what felt like a tree root and he fell flat on his face.

Both beams were on his prone body within a moment. The force of the fall had caused him to spill the paint brush and can that, up until now, he had been holding. The officers approached and one said, "Well, what have we got here?" although he was not looking at the discarded artist's gear. Instead, he had directed the beam towards Paul's foot. The thing wrapped around his ankle that had caused him to trip was not a tree root, but the brown handles of a large leather bag. Untangling Paul's foot from the valise, the policeman unzipped the bag causing some of its contents to spill onto the grass.

"Well, my lad," he said while still shining the torch onto the wall. "Grafittising Council property is a pretty serious offence on its own. But this," he continued while swishing the light onto the array of picture frames, silver clocks and jewellery now sprawled on the ground, "goes way beyond that. Where did you get this little lot from, eh?"

Paul, now completely confused, started mumbling that this was the first time he'd seen any of this stuff, but, before he had a chance to recompose himself, Horace was bellowing, "That's my, my next-door neighbour's clock. And I'm sure she has a broach exactly like that blue one just lying next to it. I told your sergeant I'd heard smashing glass. This ruffian's been breaking and entering in The Avenue! Oh, the disgrace. I want to press full charges."

But the two cops had long stopped listening to the continued hollering up above as they were now in arrest mode. One was cuffing Paul's hands behind his back, leading him out of the park and reading him his rights. The other began cordoning off the area around the perimeter of the copse with a ring of tape that read *Police Do Not Cross*.

Horace continued his screeching, trying with all his might to give the impression, on the outside, that he was the most aggrieved victim of the most heinous of crimes that had ever been committed.

On the inside, however, he could not have been more content.

Chapter Twelve

Still perched on his table and looking over the wall, Horace watched as whatever the modern-day equivalent of two panda cars bought reinforcements to the scene and the taillights of the White Maria carting Paul away vanished out of the park.

A woman he assumed to be CID seemed to take charge and instructed the assembled uniformed officers to start exploring the crime scene. However, she very quickly realised that four sets of size thirteens thrashing around in the undergrowth with just the moonlight and a quartet of torches for guidance were likely to do more harm than good, and, almost as soon as they'd started, she shouted for them to stop.

They obeyed her order immediately – almost as quickly as they did her follow-up instruction that everyone should get back to the station for a cup of tea. She directed the hapless Community Support officer, who earlier had pleaded with her to be allowed to come along for the ride but was now having second thoughts, to finish taping off the area as best he could and to guard the site as if his life depended on it. "We'll come back at 8:30 to relieve you. It should be light enough by then for us to actually see what we're doing." Spotting what she thought was a look of annoyance on the rookie's face, quipped, "See, it ain't all glamour, this job. But hey, if you get thirsty, you might find a coke or something in that old fridge."

The Councillor watched as the last of the police, baring Community Officer *Short Straw* who was now sitting on the dishwasher and kicking the fridge, had left the scene and made his way up the garden and back indoors. Horace was keen and ready to commence work on the next stage of his plan.

He started by ringing around the various journalists he knew were always interested in a story. He began by telling them that he'd been woken up in the middle of the night by a huge commotion in the park, only to find a whole battalion of police apprehending a gang of robbers they'd long suspected of ransacking houses in the area.

He happily embellished the burglary tale as much as he thought the hacks might swallow but made sure he also casually slipped in a few other nuggets he hoped they'd picked up.

"How many people in the gang did the police arrest?" asked the first reporter.

"Difficult to say." Horace told her. "It was the middle of the night after all and it was hard to see anything clearly. But in a moment when the moonlight filtered through the trees, I saw a huge mound of gold and silver valuables that must have spilled out of the gang's swag bag."

"Gosh. Brilliant!" responded the hack. "What sort of items. Jewellery?"

"Again, hard to say." said Horace. "But there was also a whole load of spray cans, paintbrushes and what have you lying around next to them. And I'll tell you another thing." he continued, trying to add some excitement and mystique to the tale. "It looks like one of them has been using all that stuff to desecrate the park-facing side of my wall. I couldn't really see exactly what had been done because, well, from where I was standing and looking over the top of the wall, everything was upside down. If I had to hazard a guess, I'd say it looked like some sort of graffiti story. Whatever it was, they'd made a huge mess; they sprayed the whole area in paint."

The silence that greeted Horace's attempt at drama from the other end of the phone was not quite the reaction he'd hoped for, so he decided to go a bit further. "If I didn't know any better," he said, pausing, for what he hoped might be to good effect, "I'd swear it looked like something that Banksy chappy might do. I know that sounds totally bizarre, and I wouldn't want to detract from the real story here about the boys in blue catching these ruffian robbers, but it sort of makes you think, doesn't it?"

That seemed to do the trick. The journalist was now fully engaged, and it took all of Horace's linguistic skills to bring the conversation to an end so that he could get on with ringing some more reporters.

By half past three, he'd finished rousing the night editor of every publication in town and, despite the adrenaline that was still coursing through his veins, felt he could manage a few hours' sleep before he had to make his next call.

Chapter Thirteen

Despite it being but a few hours since Paul Gunningham's arrest, Sargent Greig had been fending off calls from local journalists since before the sun had come up. The phone did eventually stop ringing, but only because the city's hacks had started turning up at the police station to put their questions in person. He only managed to get them to agree to leave by promising a press conference on the station's front steps.

In his hastily prepared statement, he gave them all he had: "At approximately 02:35 this morning, a 24 year old white male was arrested on suspicion of burglary in Ryelands Park. He continues to help us with our inquiries, and there will be further details released at a later date."

Unfortunately, that fell somewhat short of satisfying the baying herd.

Everyone seemed extraordinarily well informed about an event that had taken place barely half a dozen hours earlier, and despite his statement, further questions were coming thick and fast.

Who was the person arrested? Have they been charged? What stolen items had been recovered? Was there anything missing? Is it true that Banksy is the man locked up in the cells?

The policeman, not unlike his namesake, dealt with the first four queries with a pretty straight bat: We're not releasing any names at this stage; no one has been charged; details of articles found at the scene are currently being assessed; we are in the process of putting together a list of items that may have been reported missing from local properties. The fifth question, however, slightly threw the normally unflappable officer.

Banksy?" he thought. What on earth.....? His hesitancy lasted only an instant and, hoping the questioner didn't notice his momentary pause, he said, "We've got no reports of a Mr or, for that matter," hoping to inject a modicum of humour and thus deflect any further probing on the issue, "a Mrs Banksy involved in the incident." He started moving backwards, up the steps and away from the crowd, which, with the addition of a number of radio reporters and freelance photographers, had doubled in size. As he reached the sanctuary of the station's door, he called out that there would be further details to follow later today.

Once back behind his counter, he shouted for a mug of tea to be brought to him, "Right NOW!", and slumped into his chair.

As he waited for his brew to be brewed, he said to himself, "Banksy? How on earth does he fit into the equation?"

Chapter Fourteen

His radio alarm dutifully switched on at nine o'clock, gently rousing Horace with the six Greenwich time pips that marked the end of the Today programme. By the time the 9:30 news bulletin had started, Horace had drunk his coffee and felt ready to attack the next phase of *Plan H*.

Opening up the neatly folded scrap of paper he'd placed in his wallet three days earlier, he punched the number given to him by the Council's procurement team into his iPhone. Within five minutes, he'd arranged an appointment to see a Miss Dunaway of Gill, Wills, James, Farr & Andrews at 1 o'clock that afternoon.

Horace fronted up to the offices of G, W, J, F & A at 12:55 and was shown into a waiting room. "Miss Dunaway will be with you shortly." he was told by the receptionist. "Shortly" turned out to be 35 minutes later, which didn't put him in the very best of moods. However, any thoughts of aggression he may have been harvesting were soon melted away by Miss Dunaway the moment she opened the door.

LATER THAT DAY, ONCE he had returned home and was waiting for the tea to brew, Horace began reflecting on the afternoon's events.

His recollection of the initial meeting with Miss D was proving to be a bit of a haze. He had some memory that the vision, who had floated into the room over half an hour late for his appointment, had started apologising profusely for her tardiness even before she had opened the door. And when she took his hands in hers, looked into his eyes and purred, "I just can't imagine what I could possibly do to ever get you to forgive me." he simply melted away. So vague was his recall of those first few moments that he actually thought he might have momentarily blacked out – or at least lost the ability to understand English.

She was a vision. An amalgam of the best bits of Uma Thurman and Claudia Winkleman (not, Heaven forefend Horace thought, that either of them had any actual bad bits). Her hair was sandy blonde but cut with a vicious fringe that hung level with the bridge of the nose. The eyes were slightly obscured by the tresses, mascaraed in black and a half closed, but he still made out their clear and deep colour of Ukrainian blue. She was shorter than the American, taller than the Brit, but her feet (the Councillor absolutely loved feet) were all Thurman. Horace was in heaven.

But he was also there on a mission.

Horace had done his homework and knew that Vicky Dunaway was Head of Disparate Products, the department at Gill, Wills, James, Farr & Andrews that dealt with the unusual and exotic aspects of its insurance business.

As Horace moved towards one of the chairs surrounding the oak table that filled much of the room, he said, "In short, Miss Dunaway...." but she cut him off, saying, "Please, Councillor Board. Call me Vicky."

"Thank you, Vicky. And you must call me Horace." he responded, almost coherently.

"In short, Vicky," he repeated, "I think I've acquired a Banksy." Despite the fringe, Horace saw her eyes widen. He was happy to let the thought drift around in her head for a few moments and simply sat back and waited for her to respond. "A Banksy? How on earth do you *acquire* a Banksy?"

Horace told her that he had been woken up in the wee small hours of last night only to find a whole battalion of police running around every which way in the park on the other side of his wall.

"Naturally, I went to investigate and in doing so, I discovered this...." he said, handing her his iPhone. He indicated that she should scroll through the pictures. "And the entire work, every one of the twelve blocks are on my wall." He paused while she examined the photos.

"Now I'm no expert," he continued, "but I can recognise the style of one of the world's most famous street artists as well as the next man.....or woman." he added in response to the slight tilt of Vicky's head. "But to cap that off, the police told me that the chap they arrested is called Paul Gunningham."

Vicky nodded in recognition of the name. Everyone in her department, from the latest intern right up to her number two, would be familiar with the rumours of Banksy's real identity.

Horace watched as the Head of Disparate Products absorbed the pictures on his phone. "So, what do you say? On face value, it looks like I might have struck lucky. It certainly seemed worth taking the time to make this appointment and speak with an expert in the field about its legitimacy. As well, of course, to hear your advice as to what I should be doing about protecting it."

After a brief moment's thought, Vicky pressed the button on the intercom and asked the receptionist to bring in some coffee. "Do you prefer a mug or a cup, Board?" she asked before instructing her PA to ask Maria Chief, team leader of the fine and exotic arts section, to join them. It took less than thirty seconds for a well-dressed woman in her early thirties, wearing a black pencil skirt, crisp white blouse and her hair tied back in a fierce bun, to enter the room. Vicky rose and made the introductions. "Councillor Board: this is Miss Chief."

Horace avoided making any comment, although he did reflect on what a shame it was that this woman didn't work at the Council.

Within five minutes of Maria having first examined the snaps, two members of her team who specialised in street art had joined the throng, adding the weight of their opinions.

It didn't take the four insurers long to come to a consensus; chances are this was the real thing. The work of this size could be worth millions, but if it were to be insured by Gill, Wills, James, Farr & Andrews, they'd need to inspect it firsthand and protect it with every modern device known to woman. The degree of excitement in the room was well above normal levels for the insurance industry. Horace, the calmest person around the table by far, simply nodded as Miss Chief outlined the steps they'd be taking over the next twenty-four hours.

"So soon?" asked Horace. "That's extraordinarily quick."

"No time to lose, Councillor." said Maria, with just, Horace felt, a slight amount of mischief in her voice.

He returned from his reverie, lifted the cosy, poured, then stirred his tea and plonked himself in the comfiest seat in his living room. For the first time in many months, Horace began to feel that everything in his life was falling into place.

The stunning and valuable mural that he'd hoped for had been completed and was his – and his alone. All his. He'd even managed to get the Council to confirm as much in their official records. Paul Gunningham had been neatly taken out of the equation far more easily than he'd anticipated - and without the need for any great deal of input from him. The police were obliging by keeping the imposter incinerated and away from the scene, thereby stopping him from messing things up with small details like the truth. And Vicky Dunaway and Associates had convinced themselves they were dealing with a genuine Banksy.

Even the stumbling block he was particularly worried about - the small matter of where he was going to find the money to pay the insurance premium - was, in the end, hurdled without any difficulty at all.

Miss Chief had been so keen to get him signed up for their new specialist Visa credit card they'd just launched in collaboration with JP Morgan (he suspected she was on a healthy commission) that it was automatically approved. There and then. In the room. With not as much as a single question. Not only did it come on a six month's interest-free basis, but 10% of the £50,000 premium had been knocked off as a special introductory benefit. The security checks and CCTV camera that they insisted on installing (at their own expense) would be put in place the following afternoon, at which time he'd also be provided with a hard copy of the policy document.

Yes, Horace thought, everything seems to be going in the right direction. Christmas really has come early at the Councillor's home.

Chapter Fifteen

It should come as no surprise to anyone that this was not the first time Adam had been sitting at the newspaper's least popular work station. Suffice to say he knew his way around the reports on the City Council's business better than most. He had the Council's website bookmarked and the minutes for their interminably boring and tedious meetings were never more than a click away. He soon found papers for the most recent meeting, which had taken place only three days earlier.

Flicking past "Councillors in attendance", [who cares]; "Apologies for absence", [ditto]; and "Matters arising from previous meeting's minutes", [this is doing my head in], he scrolled down to what he hoped might be slightly meatier fare. *Declaration of Members' Interests* sometimes threw up an interesting nugget or two, and indeed, Adam thought he might be onto something with a note on a Councillor who, it at first appeared, might be trying to claim public funds to clean some graffiti from his wall. Alas, that little ruse seems to have been given short shrift by the Parks and Community Spaces department, so, while slightly relieved that *Cllr Can I Put My Nose In The Trough* had been told in no uncertain terms that the wall was not Council property - it belonged to him and he must take total responsibility and ownership for any scrawlings on it – this didn't offer the story he had hoped for.

Next on the agenda was the finance report, although a quick scan over the first few lines left Adam feeling less than optimistic. Blah blah street lighting repairs; blah blah cemetery hedge trimming costs; blah, blah apologies for the absence of reconciled bank statements, but the Chair confirmed that reserve funds remain at £807,067; blah, blah agreement to purchase flower bulbs for the entrance to the Royal Lancaster Infirmary in an amount not exceeding £19.99; and that was it! Blimey, Adam thought; at the last meeting they'd decided to splash £750 on some grade two listed paint to tart up the phone box that was now a library cum defibrillator store. At least that had been good for 700 words and an early knock-off!

The report on planning proved equally fruitless: not even Marina Hyde could have conjured some witty prose out of a request by the Vicar of the Second United Methodist Church for permission to demolish the outside coal bunker in the back garden of the rectory.

It was beginning to look very much as if he might be forced to trigger *Adam's Last Gasp Option*, taught to him by a journalist from *The Sun* he'd once rubbed shoulders with at some mind-numbing press conference on a subject long since forgotten. The sage advice from the old tabloid hack went along the lines of, when you're in trouble and have a deadline to make – just make something up. The more ridiculous, the better - and the less likely anyone is to question it. But just as he was about to switch into *total fabrication mode*, he spotted a familiar name under *Any Other Business*.

Sandwiched between Cllr Nyles's update on dog fouling in the cemetery and Cllr Jerry's [usual] rant on the lack of superfast broadband in Warton Parish was a comment from the local police liaison officer's report:

- PC Fivoh, the Council liaison officer, reported the Chief Inspector's recent initiative to combat fly-tipping has met with some success. The large amounts of garden waste and building rubble being dumped on roadways and public areas over recent months has abated considerably. However, since the last meeting, there has been a considerable number of kitchen appliances found abandoned around the town. PC Fivoh agreed to report back on progress in tackling this issue at the next meeting. With regards to the continuing problem of street artists in the central city area, the officer appraised the Council on the difficulties in policing this social nuisance. Like those guilty of fly-tipping dishwashers and refrigerators, the perpetrators often work under the cover of darkness and are invariably light of foot. Success in dealing with both issues is almost impossible without committing a large number of uniformed personnel to the task. However, Constable Fivoh advised that a man, believed to be a prolific sprayer of street art blighting the town, had been apprehended late last week painting a mural on a wall in Ryelands Park. In response to a question from Cllr Nyles, the officer advised that the work appeared to be based on the twelve days of Christmas. The man arrested, who was also helping them with their inquiries into a range of burglaries in the local area, is white, 24 years old and has given the name of Mr Paul Gunningham.

To many, this brief entry in the minutes would have turned very few hairs, although Adam did sense some of his quivering. Not because of the unspoken message of underfunding that the policeman was hinting at with the subtlety of a truncheon wielding copper, nor in reaction to the mention of such a well-hummed Christmas song. Get any group of people together at this time of year in the run-up to Yuletide and you'll easily generate a debate on whether it's ten ladies or Lords dancing or leaping and at least half a dozen four-part harmonies champing at the bit to bellow out the phrase, *Five Gold Rings*.

No, the tingling sensation on the back of his neck had been triggered by the mention of *Gunningham*. Admittedly, the name is perhaps slightly unusual, but it's not particularly noteworthy – at least not unless you grew up, as Adam had, on Lawrence Hill in Easton, Bristol. Anyone not familiar with this inner-city area would be unlikely to refer to Paul Gunningham in any way other than, well, Paul Gunningham. Many natives of this part of town, however, are more than likely to whisper the name Banksy.

Adam was a handful of years younger than Paul, so he hadn't really rubbed shoulders with him at Bristol Cathedral School, but by the time Banksy had painted the Mild Mild West in 1997, any Bristolian worth her or his salt was all but convinced that they knew exactly who the alter ego was.

Since then, of course, his work has become legendary – and wild wild west expensive. Adam wondered if Gunningham was indeed Banksy; what on earth was he doing touting his craft in this neck of the woods? And why would he be involved in some sort of local robberies. This could be just the 500 words he was looking for.

Chapter Sixteen

Adam felt inspired and started off with a few attempts at possible titles for his story: All I want for Christmas is a Banksy; Merry Banksy Everybody; Have yourself a merry little Banksy, and We wish you a merry Banksy were the four best of a bad bunch, though even these were, thankfully, all tossed into the discarded present pile.

Try as he might, he couldn't seem to get beyond 20th century pop songs – and progress wasn't being helped by hearing Noddy Holder's voice screaming out of every speaker in every doorway of every shop in town. However, by the time *Cum on feel the Banksy* entered his consciousness, he had an epiphany. Sod 500 hundred words - this had the makings of something far greater than a puff piece in the bottom left-hand corner of page six in the local rag.

Clearing his screen of the headlines that would have left many a sub editor screaming in pain, he switched into *ALGO mode* and rattled off what turned out to be 512 words (Ffion would surely be impressed with the provision of a dozen words over and beyond the call of duty) on an article describing how a stone carving of Pythagoras with a cherub perched on his head might have been found under a concrete coal bunker in the grounds of the Second United Methodist Church. Adam typed *Vicar locates Arch Angle* into the subject box of an email, completed his task by hitting *send* to editor@lstar.com, then opened the contacts section on his *iPhone* and started scrolling through the names, searching for forgotten friends from home.

While Adam had never actually met Paul Gunningham, he had been to his house on one occasion many many years ago, albeit not with the intention of seeing the man himself. A rumour had circulated at school (it was thought one of the older boys who had gone out with Paul's sister was behind it) that irrespective of the time of day, night, or, for that matter, year, his mother would always answer the front door dressed in an overcoat and pork pie hat. Her rationale, so the story went, was that if someone she didn't want to speak to was stood before her on the "welcome" mat, she was suitably dressed to feign being on her way out to the shops so couldn't possibly stop to chat. If, however, she was greeted by someone she was happy to meet, then she'd welcome them in, explaining her overdressed state by saying that she had just that second got in and hadn't had a chance to "even kick off me walking boots".

Adam had wanted to see for himself whether the legend had any truth in it. On his solo attempt, however, he totally failed to prove it one way or the other as instead of being greeted by Paul's mother, it was his sister, Jeanie, (*the very attractive, every adolescent teenager at school's dream*) who answered the door. After ten seconds of him just standing there, with his mouth open, looking dumb and not saying anything, she told him to bugger off and slammed it shut in his face. He didn't have the guts to try again, so he left the *Tale of the Weird Hat and Coat woman* on the shelf of unsolved mysteries.

On hearing about Adam's whimpish failure, his friend, Tim Linquist decided to have a crack at what was becoming known around the school as the Old Ma G's Mission.

Tim was one of those guys ranked well up the pecking order by his peers. Some reached such a position through strength – bullying mainly - while others attained the status less forcibly by possessing a certain sporting prowess. Tim, however, was universally looked up to for another reason. In short, he was pretty much game for absolutely anything. And no one ever really knew what he might do next. Not even his closest chums.

For example, it came as absolutely no surprise to Adam when, one Friday, after the school bell had rung for the final time that week and the two were preparing to make their way home, his mate announced he'd answered an ad in the papers from Vidal Sassoon hairdressers. They had been appealing for male models and Tim said he was going up to his salon in Covent Garden in the morning.

In total keeping with his reputation, Tim turned every single schoolboy's head the moment he walked into Mr Bradley's history lesson the following Monday.

His always vivid blonde locks had been shaped dramatically, even for Tim, into a 1920s bob. And that wasn't all. The sides of his hair were vividly coloured by streaks of yellows, greens, reds and blues that even a discerning parrot would have been proud of.

The effect was so dramatic one felt that nothing could take away from the shockingness of the coiffure – until that is you spotted he had also had his ears pierced and filled with metal hoops. At the time, this was something a great distance away from de rigueur for the male sex in general – let alone barely pubescent teenage boys. Adam always swore, when telling the tale over years to come, that the two gilded rings dangling from Tim's lobes had one word engraved on each. *Jolly* on the left and *Roger* on the right.

Mr Bradley was perhaps more exasperated than stunned. He watched as the flashes of colour and glints of gold came to rest before him and simply breathed out five words in despair: "Tim. Tim. The pirate's son."

Not long after Mr B had given him this new nickname, Tim began Operation OMG in earnest. He started by giving her doorbell a ring two or three times a week, although it took a dozen or more visits before he hit paydirt and was met by the suitably attired Mrs Gunningham. He'd been greeted on his previous attempts by young Ms G, who, by the time Tim was in double figures, had misconstrued his intentions, did a bit of flirting, and ended up getting him to ask her out on a date.

Adam had scrolled down and reached the T's in his contact list. He let the cursor rest on the entry TTTPS and pushed the *dial*. If anyone was likely to be able to shed any light on a Banksy artwork coming to Lancaster, it was *Tim Tim the Pirate's son*.

Chapter Seventeen

All four attempts at ringing Tim's number resulted in the same three pips and *failed call* notifications. Adam was a tad annoyed, but not totally surprised. People change their mobile numbers all the time and it had been, what, well over a dozen years since he'd last spoken with his exotic school friend. That aside, he wouldn't have put it past Tim to change his number every three months, just to keep everybody guessing and on their toes.

He was more successful in making contact with the next five old Bristolian chums he tried. However, all of them seemed to have followed a similar path to his own, having long left their childhood homes for the lure of London, Birmingham or Cardiff, and none had really stayed in touch with any of their teenage friends of yesteryear.

Chris Hopper gave him a number for Jeanie Gunningham and while she was happy to hear from Adam and take his call (and kindly didn't recount what a prat he'd made of himself on the one occasion they had come face to face all those years ago), she hadn't seen her childhood sweetheart for years. In fact, she told him, "The last time I saw Tim, he was behind the dodgems, snogging Anne Freakly from the upper sixth. I wouldn't have minded ordinarily, but he'd actually taken me to the fairground as his date; and I'd only nipped off to the loo for five minutes!"

Adam slumped back in his chair, letting his shoulders droop and his arms fall by his side. One out of date phone number and six dead-end leads had left him no closer to making even a modest dent in his *Tale of the Lancaster Banksy Mystery* scoop. He felt in his bones that there was a story here to be found – just not exactly what that story was (or, for that matter, where or how to find it). What he did know, however, was that he wasn't going to leave things here. Like any journalist worth their salt, he would keep digging; he just needed to find another approach.

Chapter Eighteen

The CCTV camera people had arrived on time the next day and by 16:35, an unobtrusive metal box had been wired up and installed behind one of the elephants on top of his wall. It was connected by some extraordinary and, for all Horace could tell, magical means, not only to the insurance company's recording centre, but also onto an app they'd kindly uploaded onto his iPhone. Buzz, the electrician (Horace assumed this was a quirky nickname the woman had given herself rather than a remarkable bit of foresight by her parents during the christening), showed how he could switch it on any time he fancied and look at the arial shot of the mural. "How the long winter nights might now just fly by." he joked with Buzz, trying to convey a sense of indifference rather than the total excitement he really felt.

By 17:05, Vicky had been and checked that everything was in place. She gave him the policy documents that confirmed his Gunningham/Banksy extravaganza was insured against damage and theft at its estimated market value of £5 million, but then, much to his disappointment, immediately left.

With Phases 1 (the mural was in place) and 2 (the said mural was all nice and insured) completed, Horace now needed to embark on the third part of his cunning plan and make the damn thing disappear.

He retired into the living room, plonked himself into his chair, picked up the *Lancaster Gazette* and turned to **Local Services** in the classified ads.

He'd skipped over the first eight entries, all of which had gone with the identical *Man with Van* heading. He whisked past the next four adverts, each screaming with capitals and a variety of exclamation marks like, !*NO JOB TOO SMALL!*, and gave even shorter shrift to what seemed the rather aggressive, *Give Gazza and his mates a Job! We do everything! Phone Gazza! Now! Do it!*

He hovered briefly, for obvious reasons, over *Woman: will do anything*, but while he was dwelling on exactly what that might mean, his attention was nudged towards three entries a couple of columns across that were more the sorts of things he was looking for. One, slightly more sanguine than Mr Gazza's nigh hostile tone, was headed, *Colin & Sons: Builders and Demolishers.* Next to that, although a tad more obscure, was, *If you need help, call BCH. Bob can help. Always remember. Bob can help. Just ask.* The third ad that had attracted Horace's interest was at the very bottom of the page. It read, *Pat's Perfect PO Box.*

Yes, thought Horace. They should all do very nicely.

Chapter 19

Inserting an anonymous pay-as-you-go Sim card he had purchased that afternoon (anonymously, using cash, obviously) into his phone, Horace dialled one of the numbers he'd circled in the local rag and waited. It was answered with a short and simple "Yes?".

After four or five seconds of total silence, Horace realised the young woman (even though he only had one syllable to work with, he was pretty confident he was talking to someone female and still in their twenties) was waiting for him to continue the conversation. "I'm responding to your advertisement in the *Gazette*. I believe you're happy to do *anything*?"

The phone went dead.

Reflecting that he probably went a little more husky on the, *anything,* than might be considered appropriate, Horace redialled. As soon as he heard the monosyllabic response, he jumped straight in, saying he had just that second rung, he was terribly sorry, he could probably have worded his introduction a little more tactfully and that he really did have a job he needed doing. "I can assure you," he said. "Everything is absolutely and totally above board."

Although no response was forthcoming, she at least hadn't cut him off again, so he continued, "Nothing sordid." Silence. "All quite decent". Still nothing. "Certainly no, Hanky-Panky.".

That last phrase seemed to do the trick. Once the voice on the other end had stopped laughing, he heard dialogue. "Sorry." Then the voice said, "The advert is deliberately worded to attract attention, but it does mean I have to screen out a whole load of unwanted nutters, sex pests and smart Alecks it inevitably generates. I can usually pick out the wrong 'uns by some of the terms they use. *Hanky-panky* has never been one of them, so what do you have in mind?"

Horace explained that he had some building work he wanted done to his wall: "It's basically getting rid of a whole load of graffiti, but chemicals won't shift it. The brickwork or plaster will have to be taken off. I doubt it's particularly complicated." he said. "Once a builder's seen what's involved, I'm sure it won't take anyone worth her or his salt more than a couple of minutes to work out what needs to be done. My problem is that I'll be out of town for the next few weeks, so I need someone to engage the tradespeople for me. Does that fall in the *unsordid enough* category for you?", Horace said, trying to inject a modicum of humour into the conversation.

"Go on." the voice encouraged.

Horace told her of the possible contacts he'd found in the Gazette's local ads, leading off with *Colin & Sons,* as he thought they looked the most likely candidates and a decent sort of outfit. "It's a local firm. If you've got a pen," he said, "I'll give you their name and phone number. You might as well sort everything out from start to finish. Don't overcomplicate it; just tell them it's your problem and you want it to go away. That way, it gives you the authority to make any decisions without them saying they wanted to speak with the boss on any issues that cropped up. It shouldn't take you more than an hour or so to meet up with them and agree on the work and the price. I'm reckoning on having to pay upwards of £1,000 for the job – and I'll pay you, what shall we say, £100 for your contribution?"

Horace was slightly relieved that this at last prompted a more expansive reaction, although he was disappointed at being forced to up his go-between's side of the deal by 500 percent before she finally agreed to take on the task. "Well, that's certainly a lot more than I'd anticipated paying, but I suppose...", Horace thought for a few moments before finally agreeing to her terms, albeit with a modest caveat. "OK," he said. "£500 for you and up to £1,000 for the job. But you sort everything out up front. I'll pay you half now, the other half once the job's done."

He gave her the location of the wall in the park. "Give me a call once you've got it sorted and settled on the price for the job itself and I'll have someone meet you with the £750. I presume you're happy with cash money?"

"Used twenties and tens would do very nicely." She replied.

He was just about to finish the conversation when it suddenly hit him. "Oh, by the way. I've just realised. I don't know what to call you. What's your name?"

"My name?" the voice said, "is Joan, but everyone calls me Jean. Don't ask me why. Jean Happs. And you better not mess me around. Until that £750 is in my hands, I ain't taking this caper any further or speaking to no one."

Horace wondered momentarily if Jean, or Joan, or whoever it was he was speaking with had wandered into gang land New York, but he assured her there would be no problem on the money side of things. As he ended the call, he said to himself, "Well, Miss Happs. Let's hope you don't have any while sorting everything out for me."

Chapter 20

Boyed with some optimism that has been seriously lacking in Horace's life for some time, he logged onto BungaBungaBunga.com, a new payday loan website he hadn't targeted before. He'd been keeping it in reserve and, despite the immense temptation, untouched in case the need arose for immediate cash. This, Horace reasoned, was such a moment and a mere six hours after inputting some slightly dubious details online, £750 had been couriered to his front door in Primary Avenue.

It came in a robust, A4 and rather garish, Horace thought, red envelope. It initially struck him as being a more appropriate container for a Christmas card, but he then wondered if *Bungabungabunga.com* were sending out cerebral messages: This is money provided on an overdraft. This is *red* money.

While waiting for the cash to arrive, Horace had made two phone calls.

The first was to someone who'd answered his call as "Patrick. I'm Patrick, the PO Box person."

At first, Horace found Patrick to be very helpful. He started by explaining how their facility usually worked. "You pop in, we take a few details, give you a key and Bob's your uncle. You can access your pigeonhole – we like to call them that; it sounds a bit quirky, don't you think – anytime, day or night.

Horace actually thought that calling a PO Box a *pigeonhole* sounded more naff than quirky, but he wasn't yet feeling the need to downgrade his opinion of postman Pat. Not quite yet, anyway.

"I'm afraid I was looking for something a little more flexible. You see, I'm going to be dropping things off for someone else to collect, and I was planning to deposit my first package early tomorrow, before you open and too soon to get a key to him."

"Ah." said Pat. "I think *Pat's PO Box Password Programme* is just the thing for you and your colleague. If you could pop into our shop," Horace felt there was a little more *popping in* required than he'd have ideally liked, but stopped short of saying anything, "and open an account; I can set things up while you're here. We could agree on a password and then, when your partner pops in," Horace winced again, but still said nothing. "as long as he knows the right words to say, we'll give him the key that will let him pop your box open."

Horace felt the time had arrived to say something, but Patrick carried on obliviously and said, "Actually, if you give me your bank card details, I can set everything up for you now."

Which is what Horace did: first reading out the numbers on the only active card in his possession, then settling on *Christmas* as the password.

Quickly bidding Pat farewell before he had a chance to pop the kettle on or something, he pressed the red button on his mobile and immediately dialled the second number on his list.

His call was answered, not with the usual *hello* or some such greeting, but with some words Horace recalled seeing in the *Gazette*. "BCH. Always remember. Bob can help, so Hi, and how can Bob help?"

Horace thought he could hear some fairground music in the background, but leaving that to one side, he said, "I need someone to collect an envelope from a Post Office Box and deliver it to a woman sitting on a bench in Ryelands Park." He paused, half expecting some sort of response, but when none came, said, "Hello. Are you there? Did you hear me?"

Deathly silence ensued. Horace was just about to give up and hang up when he heard Bob say, slowly and deliberately, "You want me to collect an envelope from a Post Office Box?"

"Yes," said Horace. "Quite right."

It seemed a lifetime until Bob spoke again, but any relief that Horace might have felt from hearing there was life at the end of the phone soon turned to frustration as Bob proceeded to repeat the instructions back to him, line by line.

"And then you want me to take this envelope into Ryelands Park?"

"Precisely".

"And go to a woman sitting on a bench?"

"Bingo."

"And give her the envelope?"

"Super. I'm glad to see you've got the gist of it. But one more thing: Do you have a camera?"

Bob replied, a fraction quicker this time, though not as much as Horace really noticed, "You want to know if I have a camera?"

Horace half kicked himself for not predicting and thereby heading off this latest line of enquiry, but held back. He was hopeful the end of the conversation must surely be within reach, so persevered. "Exactly. Because I want you to take a photograph of the woman holding the envelope after you've given it to her."

"Well." said Bob, almost immediately. "I could hardly take a photograph of her holding the envelope *before* I'd given it to her, could I?"

It took the Councillor the same amount of time as the first part of their conversation to read over the address of the PO Box company and then explain why Bob needed to say *Christmas* to a chap he'd never met called Pat. But by the time Bob had repeated, "I go up to the counter and say, Christmas?" for the third time, Horace felt confident he'd grasped what was required. And that he was ideally suited for the task.

He had intended to ask for a copy of the photo confirming the money had been handed over to Jean to be taken back and left at the PO Box. However, he didn't feel he could face a further half-hour doing another couple of rounds while that additional task was clarified. No, he thought. Hopefully, the mere taking of the photograph would be enough to stop Jean from potentially gumming up the works by making any claim of non-receipt of funds. He only needed her to be happy for a few days – at least until she'd sorted out the task he'd given her.

OK, thought Horace. Maybe the guy does sound slightly dim, to say the least, but he'd conveyed an air of confidence that he was capable of picking up an envelope and handing it over to the intended recipient without incident. Horace was sure that, unless he specifically told Bob to look inside the envelope, he wouldn't. Likewise, so long as the words "make certain you lose it before you get to the bench" were not uttered, then Bob was unlikely to misplace the package *en route*.

Jean had texted Horace's secret phone, telling him she was arranging to meet the builders in the morning and that he should make sure the cash was in her hands before they turned up.

It was all a bit rushed. He'd have liked a chance to put *BCH Bob* to the test before sending him out into a live situation. But needs must. So, he told Bob there would be two envelopes ready for his collection by 7:00 a.m. "One will be unsealed with your £50 fee inside. The other will be stuck down. That's the one you take to the woman in the park." He explained the exact location of the bench where Jean would be sitting and finished off with, "She'll be expecting you."

When Bob said, "Leave it to me. It's all a bit like the Pink Panther, isn't it?" Horace wondered, not for the first time during this conversation, whether he should hang up and look for another courier. But he'd gone this far, and Bob knew everything about the drop. Even the magic password. He decided, therefore, to carry on, as Sid James might have said, regardless. But he might also hang around outside the PO Box place; make sure Bob did actually turn up and then follow him to the park. Just to be sure. The envelope he'd be delivering may only contain £750, but £5 million rested on it being delivered to Miss Happs, and he certainly didn't want any of those.

Chapter 21

Jean rang the number Horace had given her. An absolutely charming receptionist answered the phone, told her she was speaking with Caroline Gnomer and asked how she could help.

"Well, Miss Gnomer, someone has grafittised my garden wall along the north side of Ryelands Park. Apparently, you can't get the paint off with any recognised agent, so I'm calling to see if your firm might be able to hack the offending doodling off the brickwork and return it to its previous pristine state."

Caroline said that this sounded exactly like the sort of work Colin & Sons would undertake. "We do a lot of work in and around the park; when would it be convenient for the four partners to come along and see the task firsthand? How does first thing tomorrow sound?"

"Four partners?" queried Jean. "Couldn't the boss, Colin himself, just pop over on his own to have a quick look first before sending the cavalry in?"

"No, I'm afraid not." the receptionist replied. "There's no Mr Colin Senior involved in the firm anymore. It's just his four sons now and they never go anywhere without each other. This really is a true family business. I'm the only *outsider* they've ever employed – and that's just because I was the boys' nanny. They grew up with me in Carnforth after the family left Iceland following the Cod Wars."

Horace had said that he wanted the work to be carried out as unobtrusively as possible: *With the minimum amount of fuss and the least amount of noticeable activity, Miss Happs* were his closing instructions. Whatever was behind this directive, Jean wasn't sure. She guessed his intention was for her to organise something somewhat lower-key than having a trowel (or whatever the collective noun of builders is) of four labourers stomping around in the open where they could be easily seen and their presence equally easily remembered. However, she'd already given the game away on the location [a rookie mistake, she thought, chastising herself], so she felt little option other than to continue.

THE FOLLOWING MORNING, Jean was sitting on Dennis's bench, waiting. She was flicking through a bundle of ten and twenty-pound notes that some chap called Bob had just handed to her.

Funny chap, Bob, she thought to herself as he walked away. He didn't even ask me my name. He appeared out of nowhere with a camera strapped around his neck, handed me the package I was sort of expecting and said, "There you go. I knew Bob could help. Always remember. BCH. Bob can help. Just ask". Then, not bothering to explain or wait for any form of response, he grasped his camera, took my picture, backed away and left.

Bob had delivered the money in a bright red envelope, the sort that would perhaps more usually be used for concealing a Valentine's Day card. Jean thought she'd be happy to forsake all future traditional missives of love if they could be replaced with ones containing cash money.

Satisfied that she was now exactly £750 richer, she bent the envelope in half and slid it into a fold within her handbag. Clipping the clasp shut, she looked up just in time to see four men turning off the path running along the far side of the park and starting to walk in her general direction. As they strode towards her, Jean was struck by the fact that their strides were in unison, as if they were marching in sync with each other. They were all of similar, if not equal, height. As they neared to within a few dozen yards, she could see that they were dressed identically: collarless shirts, green with red hoops beneath donkey jackets, blue and unbuttoned; corduroy trousers, khaki with turn-ups; and Dr Martin boots, each one of the eight toe caps stained with what looked like dried cement. All four of them were carrying tartan bags slung over their shoulders, with the strap diagonally across their chests holding the jackets in place. It gave the appearance that they were each sporting a military sash. As they drew nearer, Jean realised that what she had assumed to be four (identical) copper-coloured berets were in fact not hats at all. Each man had a dramatic shock of deep amber hair, cut in a style *The Beatles* would have been proud of back in the day.

They approached Jean in a perfect row and, as if by command, stopped within touching distance of the seated Miss Happs. The man on the left edge of the party extended his right arm and said, "Jean? Jean Happs? I'm Colin. Colin Smith. Nice to meet you."

Jean was slightly taken aback. "But I thought your receptionist said Colin Smith no longer worked for your company, or was that a misnomer?"

"That is indeed her name," replied Colin, "but no, you are correct; my father passed away a few years ago. I was named after him."

Anyone meeting the offspring of Mr and Mrs Smith, a pleasant and devoted couple originally from Reykjavik in Iceland, for the first time soon becomes aware they have several distinguishing traits. Within moments, however, almost everyone seems to focus on four specific characteristics.

First off, they are quadruplets. No doubting that. Their mother, had she been present, could certainly have vouched for that, no question. She'd been admitted to the hospital at the first twinge of labour at one minute past midnight on the 19th September and, barely four minutes later, Smith number one was born. His three siblings, however, weren't quite so eager to see the light of day and held back, prompting the second most prominent fact about the quads: they were all born on different days.

The second eldest arrived on September the 20th; the third could not be lightly tapped on the bottom until the 21st; and it wasn't until the 22nd, by which time the original medical team, who had been on duty when Mrs S first took up residence in the ward earlier in the week and whose shift had come around again, that numero four deigned to make an appearance.

The third most notable thing about the brothers was that, despite it appearing on all their schoolwork - and even being stitched onto the labels of each and every garment they ever wore - their surname wasn't Smith at all. It was Fugl. The rebranding occurred on their first day at West Cliff Primary School.

The brothers had been placed in the class of Mr Bonkersley, a local schoolteacher in the northeast of England where men are men and vowels are often dispensed with. He was a true Yorkshire lad, born and bred. Mr B didn't suffer fools, gladly or otherwise and his default position when presented with any problem he couldn't deal with, was to power through with no real thought about the implications.

It was the first day of a new academic year. His new class of fresh-faced young learners were looking up, in awe, at their new master, waiting eagerly for their register to be taken. And it was at this moment, in these brand new and wide-eyed surroundings, that the assembled group were treated to an early example of what they would all come to learn was the renowned *Bonkersley Bluster*.

He had whisked through the first few names on the register: Jimmy Atkinson, Beatrice Barlow, Wendy Crooks and Brian Edwards with barely a pause for breath. On reaching the next group of students on his list, however, the teacher was brought to an abrupt stop. Staring at him from off the page were four names under *F*: Fugl. Mr Bonkersley had been made aware that this year he would be teaching a set of quads and that they originated from somewhere in Scandinavia, but he was in no way prepared for the fact that he might not have the faintest idea how to say their surname.

To be fair, it wasn't the easiest of Nordic names to be presented with. In Oslo, it would be pronounced *foolce*, while in their native Iceland, it was more like *fooks*. The Norwegians and Swedes have their own variations, although, one doubts, even if he had been aware of that, such knowledge was likely to have helped him out. To Bonkersley's credit, he did give it a reasonable go. He tried Fogal, then Fugel Finlignorton, Foogatine and Fourgla, none of which met with any form of recognition from the boys. He even gave Forglington a bash, although this was clearly more in desperation than any real expectation of success. After several more failed attempts, the teacher concluded he was unlikely to ever hurdle this family name with any great success. Nor did he have any intention of trying to do so on a daily basis. Instead, he came up with a suitable English, nay, pet, God's own country alternative and, from that moment forth, they universally became known as *The Smiths*.

The fourth detail about the boys, however, was the one that stuck in the minds of most people who met them. It was not that they had different surnames from the ones printed on their passports, nor that they were quadruplets who weren't born on the same day. No. As interesting as these other quirks were, there was one thing that anyone who had ever met the boys remembered. They were all called Colin.

Most people stumble on this peculiarity almost immediately on meeting the Smiths, and, as the other three chaps standing before her by the park bench each followed their (she later discovered) eldest brother's lead, extending their hands to her in similar fashion and saying, "Please, call me Colin.", Jean was no different.

The moment she said, "So you are all called Colin?" the conversation was destined to follow a well-trodden path.

As one, the boys replied, "Yes." Then continuing, if not in four-part harmony, in unison, "Our father was a big fan of George Foreman." in such a way that suggested they felt this information was sufficient to clarify the issue without the need for further explanation.

Jean stared back with the glazed expression of a woman not completely on the same page as them, but was keen to move the conversation on to the reason they were here, so she was happy to risk remaining unenlightened.

Pointing at Colin #one, to her left, she said, "Let me show you exactly what I need doing. Your brothers can come and follow on behind." (which they proceeded to do – and while keeping perfect step with each other). She led them through the copse, pausing as they reached the wall. With a sweeping motion of her arm, she pointed out what Horace had called *the offending artwork and affront to my property.*'

"I want this lot gone and replaced with, maybe, a fresh skin of plaster? What do you reckon? Half a day's work at most - £100 cash all in?"

Now, while conversations with these lads often lead to one being left with the impression that their social skills were somewhat lacking (which invariably they were), when it came to matters of business, you would never find four sharper pins in the sewing box.

Colin #two was an electronics geek. He had already clocked the CCTV camera behind what looked like to him a Disney Dumbo character on top of the wall. It was pointing down in their general direction, causing him to wonder why such surveillance might be necessary in a scrubby area behind an out of the way bench on the edge of a park.

Colin #three (an expert in town planning regulations) knew that, while this wall may be owned by the the woman standing in front of them, a permanent structure bordering a public space is automatically deemed Grade 2 listed and special permissions would be needed before they would be able to carry out any work on it whatsoever.

Colin #four's attention was elsewhere. As the brother in charge of logistics, he was already anticipating the problems they'd encounter getting the necessary skip and cement mixing equipment to this corner of a recreation area so far away from any roadway. His assessment was that this was going to be less than straightforward (which is a standard building euphemism for "more expensive than you think, Guv'nor").

Returning to the eldest sibling (a degree in communications from Edinburgh University), although he was giving Jean the air of someone mulling over the job, he was in fact concentrating more on the expressions on his brothers' faces. He'd seen these grimaces before and, as if by osmosis, understood what each was thinking. I'm afraid, Miss Happs, that I don't think we're going to be able to help you on this. Let's just say that we are a long way apart on the likely cost of this job and, even with the very best will in the world, I doubt either of us will find an acceptable figure we'd both be happy with. Colin and Sons would like to thank you for your interest, and I hope we will be able to be of some service to you sometime in the future."

As dismissive as his remarks were, Colin (#one) said them with a twinkle in his eye and a softness in his tone. He carefully took Jean's hand in his and kissed it gently before, equally carefully, returning it to her side.

And then, as one, the four men turned on their heels and, with their backs now to Jean, proceeded to walk in an age-appropriate single file through the copse. Once out into the open, they reformed into line, side-by-side and strode away, each in perfect step with one another, back in the direction from which they came.

Jean watched as the four builders left the park.

She was a bit taken aback by the way her proposal had been pretty much rejected out of hand, but perhaps only offering ten percent of what the Councillor had authorised she could go up to was a mistake. Oh well, she thought; onto plan B.

Chapter 22

In contrast to Colin & Sons, Gazza and his mates did not have an ex-nanny as their receptionist to field calls. Actually, they didn't have a receptionist at all. Instead, Jean was greeted by a man who, without so much as a by your leave or how's your father, simply said, "Gazza will buzza ya back." and the phone line going dead.

She had drawn a total blank in trying to make contact with any of the Councillor's other three suggestions: *Brick it and Associates: we'll do anything and at the drop of a hat* (weren't available for three months); *Honest John's building works: no job too small* (they were not interested in a simple day task); and *AAA Anyjob: we are available for you 24/7* (they weren't answering the phone).

This had left Jean now staring at her handset, with the sinking feeling this fifth and final option was not looking hopeful. But then her phone rang and, much to Jean's surprise, it was Gazza, buzzing back as promised.

Jean told him she had some graffiti that she wanted removed off her wall and arranged to meet him (with or without his mates; she wasn't quite sure whether they'd be coming) at two o'clock that afternoon. She started describing the location, only to be stopped at the mention of Dennis's bench. "I know it well, luv." Gazza said, and Jean somehow sensed a wink and a nod of his head. "You say no more. I'll see you there at two."

As the line went dead, Jean felt pangs of both optimism and concern. Sure, she'd found someone else to come and check out the task, but Gazza's apparent lack of curiosity worried her. He hadn't bothered to question what the job might be or how much it might pay, but still seemed more than happy to drop everything and meet up with a total stranger in some God-forsaken corner of the park.

Still, by half past one, Jean was sat on the bench, tucking into a *Big Mac* lunch she'd picked up on the way. Staring out in the general direction she'd seen the Smith boys cross the park towards her that morning. Suddenly she was grabbed around the waste from behind by someone who simultaneously yelled, "Gotcha!" in her right ear.

She jumped out of her skin and onto the grass, sending her medium fries and caramel iced frappé flying. Looking up through the slats in the bench, she saw a tall, lean young guy, late teens/early twenties, with a stunning shock of white bleached hair, pointing down at her and laughing uncontrollably. He was wearing a black trench coat, unbuttoned and revealing a red polo shirt and a yellow tartan scarf with matching trousers. He reminded her of someone Mary Tourtel might have brought to a party.

"Sorry, luv." he said, his laughter having subsided. "I really didn't mean to scare you. I just saw you there, Big Mac in one hand, some nobby-looking drink in the other and..........I couldn't resist. Didn't mean any harm. I'm here for the job, by the way – but you probably guessed that?"

As Jean began to regain her composure, she wondered what on earth made this guy, whoever the hell he was, believe she could have possibly guessed such a thing. Her second thought was that she'd like to smash the remnants of the *MacSpecial lunch* she was still holding deep into this bloke's face, but Dennis's bench was in the way which sort of diffused the moment. Instead, she settled on, "Who are you and what on earth are you doing here?"

Blonde hair, yellow trouser man looking down and, as if absolutely nothing untoward had just taken place, said, "My name's Barry. Bazza for short, but me mates call me Rupert. Not really sure why. Anyway, Gazza couldn't make it. I'm here to price up the job for him. What do you want doing?"

Dropping her hamburger onto the ground to join the bag of half-eaten fries, she pushed Bazza, or Rupert, or whatever his name was through the copse, between the fridge freezer and dishwasher, bypassing a large pool of some brown gooey mess that must have emulated from one of the appliances and up to the wall, where she began explaining what she wanted doing.

"Well." said Rupert once she'd outlined the job. "That doesn't seem like much of a problem at all. Actually, it looks like a whole load of fun. Hack off these bits, chip off those bits; slap a bit of plaster here, a bit of plaster there, lick of paint here, lick of paint there, lick o' paint, lick o' paint, everywhere some lick o' paint." Rupert turned, looked at Jean with an attempt at a flirty smile, thinking his quaint little summary of the job might have melted her a bit. Perhaps even made her warm to him.

From Jean's unflinching stare, Rupert soon realised he was some considerable way away from being anywhere near correct.

"Well," said Jean without the trace of a smile or so much as the nod of encouragement, "if it's as straightforward as you make it sound, it shouldn't take too long or cost too much, should it?"

Rupert, sensing the tone and realising he really wasn't going to get anywhere near first base with this one, decided to go into *teeth-sucking business* mode.

"Well.... three of us, a couple of barrows, a few picks and shovels.....a bit of slap....done in a day: £300 a corner plus fifty quid for eventualities, so nine fifty, all in, cash, no VAT, no questions asked. Or answered." he winked, in one last desperate effort to break her down.

While Jean had no intention of dropping her guard before the numbskull in front of her, he'd just come in at £50 below her limit and given this was also the only bid she had and was likely to get for the job, she smiled and said, "Done. When can you get it sorted?"

Chapter 23

Gazza didn't believe in coincidences.

As he pressed the *end call* button on his phone, terminating his conversation with Jean, he frowned slightly and stared out the grubby window on the side of the dilapidated caravan he liked to refer to as his office.

This was the third *cold* call he'd taken in as many hours looking for him to sort out some problem or other with graffiti. The first enquiry raised not so much as a hair on the back of his neck: perhaps someone had seen the number on the side of his van and gave it a call on spec. The second time a similar potential job rang through, his suspicious nature was more nudged than aroused, although he soon shrugged that off with the thought maybe the cost of the advert in the *Gazette* (which he'd decided to do more because he felt an affinity with the name of the rag rather than holding out any realistic expectation of it generating any work) had borne fruit after all. Perhaps, he argued to himself, he should just count his blessings rather than generate conspiracy theories. But this third call began to stretch the idea that this might simply be good fortune falling in his lap. Usually, any fortune that did land in that vicinity tended to be some considerable distance away from being good. And anyway. Gazza didn't believe in coincidences.

In the yard in front of him stood a variety of 40 or 50 clapped-out dishwashers, washing machines, microwaves and refrigerators. All were lined up and neatly positioned, much like a platoon of soldiers waiting to be given their instructions to dismiss. One of Gazza's sidelines (he actually had so many of these that it was sometimes difficult to work out what they were on the side of) was to collect and dispose of unwanted white goods. While the number ready for dispatch had built up to such a degree that he really should be sorting them out as a matter of priority, they could remain where they were – at least for the moment.

He'd been working a lot in "the upper Westside" or "Castle Heights" areas of Lancaster, pretentious names conjured up by local estate agents rather than ones you'd be able to locate on a map. But these labels had gradually been adopted by the upwardly mobile (or YUPPIES, as Gazza might have called them in his younger days), keen to buy into their hype and propagate their myth. One common thread among these aspiring yet common people was their desire to stamp their own authority on their new properties, and this was where *yours truly* had become involved.

With the government's simplification of permitted development rights in 2015, allowing homeowners greater flexibility to undertake modest domestic modifications without having to undertake formal planning applications, came the rush of demand for extensions and patios, particularly in these more affluent areas of the city. And when the one or two established building firms could no longer cope with the clamour for their services, *Gazza & Sons Conservatories* had sprung up, almost out of nowhere, to help fill the gap. Similar cravings for garages to be knocked through and kitchens refurbished were soon being dealt with by a variety of hastily created firms, of which *Gazza & Sons Conversions* and *Gazza & Sons Dining Services* were but two.

Gazza was a little bit of a Del Boy, but he wasn't stupid enough to kill any golden gift horse laying any egg or looking him in the mouth. He made sure he did a job well enough not to require any great deal of follow-up work or snagging and this, together with his low overheads and equally low prices, led to his services being well spoken of and much in demand.

The white goods disposal line (undertaken by *Gazza & Sons Clearances*) came about as a by-product of all this work. On his first ever kitchen job in *Lancs Park*, the punter had begged him to sort out the disposal of the old fridge freezer and dishwasher he was replacing. This hadn't been part of the original deal, but after much whining and pleading, Gazza reluctantly agreed to take them away. Of course, for *reluctantly*, read *for a suitable fee*.

"You just don't know how difficult it is to get rid of these things, governor. The Council won't take take 'em off you. Tell you what: you give me an extra 50 notes an item and I can make 'em disappear for you. I'll dispose of them with care and consideration. You can rely on me."

Of course, neither consideration nor care came into the equation for this particular sort of task. Gazza had decided early on that any old, out-of-way ditch would be a cheap and good enough resting place for these clapped-out old machines.

However, as he drove away from a quiet side street off the Morcombe Road, having left the white goods behind him and thinking what an easy *one off* way this was to have picked up a hundred quid, tax-free with no questions needing to be answered, little did he realise just what a very nice little earner this line of business was about to become.

Whether it was by word of mouth, a load of people seeing him shove an old Siemens into his van, or the Council closing down completely their domestic removal services, he had no idea. He just knew that within days he was inundated with calls virtually begging him to provide a similar disposal service. Inside a week, he had a list the length of his office of addresses with Boshes and Indesets that the owners wanted to see the back of and who were all quite happy to pay him £50 a go for his trouble.

This had all happened over the course of the last twelve months. Right now though, his concentration was on the dialogue he'd just had with, well......who the woman on the phone really was; he wasn't quite sure. What he did know, however, was that something wasn't quite right.

He'd begun to sniff a rat when Jean had proposed he meet her in a quiet corner of the park and started to try and pinpoint the place by reference to an old bench. Without her saying another word. Gazza knew exactly the location she was talking about. It had been less than a week since he'd sat on that bench, sweat dripping from his brow, having just carted and dumped a washing machine, fridge freezer and dishwasher right next to it. He remembered the dedication to Dennis in 1964, as it was his father's name and the year he had passed away. He remembered thinking at the time that this was exactly the sort of coincidence he'd learned to be wary of and he had even had half a thought of reloading the white goods in the van and finding a different final resting spot for them. But by God, were they heavy and Rupert was moaning about having to get back to the dry cleaners to pick up his spare pair of yellow tartan trousers before they closed, so he decided, against his better judgement, to leave them where they were.

But now he was in a quandary. Was this some kind of trap, or could it just possibly be the one thing he found it so hard to accept: a simple, unconnected piece of chance? He'd been so careful in selecting the places and timings for the dumpings: no busy locations and always under the convenient cover of thick vegetation and darkness. He couldn't, in a month of Tuesday's believe he'd been found out. Or was this all just wishful thinking? There was surely no way this Jean's call could be unrelated to his illegal fly-tipping, could it? Perhaps this woman was working for the Council? Maybe they'd somehow managed to pull together a list of his other *deposits* and were now looking to confront him in person at the most recent scene of one of his crimes? Local Authority fines of one thousand pounds per item was something he certainly didn't want to think about.

His inclination was to forget about this Jean and walk away. If it was, after all, just a coincidence, then the only thing he'd lose was the opportunity of a bit of easy money cleaning some graffiti off an old dear's wall. But if they really were onto him, then they already had his number and burying his head in the sand would neither change the situation nor stop him from looking over his shoulder for evermore.

He stared back out at the army of white kitchen appliances in his yard, all standing in line and waiting for disposal. While they remained here, he remained vulnerable. They needed shifting sooner rather than later. But was he in a position to do that in a safe and measured way, or was he in such a dodgy pickle that caution had to be immediately thrown into the ether and his boys called in to undertake a speedy evacuation.

After a few moments thought, he decided to go down the optimistic route. He'd find out exactly what the authorities knew or didn't know before planning his next move. After some deliberation, he decided Rupert should be the one to try and get the lowdown on the situation. If the Council did know about his little scam, better the *Tartan Bear* be caught than him. In the meantime, it wouldn't hurt to call his lads over so they could start working on getting rid of the rest of the incriminating evidence.

Gazza didn't believe in coincidences. But that wasn't stopping him from secretly praying that, on this occasion, one did exist.

Chapter 24

Gazza's three sons, Dougal, Dylan and Brian (Mrs Gazza, Flo, or Florence for long, had grown up on 1960's children's TV and loved Jasper Carrot) were huddled around the small table in the centre of the caravan. They'd answered their dad's call almost immediately and for the last hour, had been pouring over a map of Lancaster and its surrounding areas.

Their father's instructions when this fly-tipping business first started was for an admonitory approach to finding a spot to offload the surplus kitchenalia. However, not really understanding what that meant, they developed their own tactics of driving down a road, checking no one was looking, pushing the stuff out the back of the van and zooming off at high speed. By the time Gazza had found out, there were freezers and fidges dotted all around the town, and there was no going back.

For the mass evacuation of his yard that faced them now, though, Gazza insisted on a much more structured plan. Coloured pins had therefore been distributed to his boys with the instruction that they should be stuck in the city's various *out of the way* spots that the collective was sure (or, at least, hopeful) they hadn't used before.

They'd completed this task in worryingly quick time, so, in advance of them hitting the highway to carry out what the middle son insisted on calling *Operation White Wash Clear Out* (Dylan always liked to add a sense of drama wherever he could), Gazza thought it best to at least glance at the map and check the proposed ports of call his lads had come up with.

He immediately saw the necessity to pluck out the three pins he'd presumed Dylan – it was bound to have been Dylan – had stuck in the mayor's extensive back garden. In a somewhat despairing tone, he asked Dylan what on earth he thought he was doing. It was plainly rhetorical, so his son's response of "Living the dream, dad, living the dream." didn't progress things all that far.

Hoping he'd taken the most likely mistakes out of the equation, Gazza shooed his offspring out of his office, Fagin style, wishing them all well as they left and hoping they'd be back soon. In truth, his only realistic hope was that the dark winter night would make up for their lack of stealth and nouse.

As his brood pulled out of the yard with a number of the regiment of white goods loaded onto the battered, non-liveried van they used for these purposes, the headlights landed on someone limping across the gravel towards the caravan.

As soon as the figure triggered the security light bolted above the doorway, he saw at once that it was Rupert, and what a sorry state he looked. In addition to dragging his right leg behind the rest of his body, one hell of a bruise was circling his left eye. And the pair of his usually immaculate yellow trousers looked as if they'd been dragged through a mud bath.

Gazza shepherded him into the office. Rupert just stood by the table, gently rubbing the side of his face but concentrating more on the state of his apparel. "And it was the first time I'd worn them since picking 'em up from the dry cleaners the other day!"

Gazza covered the nearest seat with newspaper before motioning the sobbing shape before him to sit. Resting a hand on his shoulder, he softly said, "Barry." He thought this was one of those situations where he should go with the name his mother might use in order to gain the maximum response. "Tell me. What happened?"

Rupert detailed his meeting with Jean in the park, including mentioning that she led him "….right by a spot where we'd dumped a couple of washing machines or the like only the other week. Who'd have thought it?" He shrugged his shoulders and tossed a quizzical look across the table. When his question prompted nothing beyond a scowl, he decided best just to continue.

He told Gazza all about the wall and the numbered drawings and pictures on twelve sections of it and how this Jean just wanted it all to be gotten rid of; cut back to the brickwork. "I had a good shifty round and it really didn't look too much of a tricky job at all. Here, have a look at this." Rupert took out his phone and started swiping through some photos. "Here's the whole area. See how the wall is portioned up with what looks like individual blocks? Well, each of these paintings is on a separate one of those. Anyway, I barely touched this one along the bottom – the one with the yellow cartoon canaries and the number four in the corner. I had my screwdriver in my hand and, I swear, I barely touched it – and it just came away from the brickwork. Look. There it is, just resting on the grass."

Gazza motioned for him to carry on. Rupert said that he gave another square a tap, "Number five. It had some sort of snow scene on it. And I could see that it wouldn't take much more to make that one come away either. I thought this job's gonna be a breeze. One of us could have it done in an hour. And then I remembered what you'd taught me."

Gazza hated to think what on earth he was going to hear next, but sat quietly, albeit more in hope than expectation.

"You always said that if you get called out on a job, that looks like a piece of cake – and smells like a piece of cake - then the chances are the person that's offering it to you don't have a clue what a tasty piece of cake they're trying to give you. In short, they probably have no idea just how straight-forward the job really is, so dive in, chance your arm, and quadruple the price. Which is exactly what I did!"

Gazza looked at Rupert, staring across the table with an expression of satisfaction that even Mick Jagger would have been proud of. "But what on earth happened to your face?" he asked. "And your leg? And your trousers?"

Rupert's air of jubilation vanished as he involuntarily moved his left hand up to gently caress his eye. "Well." he started. "This girl, Jean. I'd taken a bit of a shine to her. She'd been playing it cool with me up until then, but I knew she really fancied me; she kept sending out all these messages. Anyway, after the yellow birds had fallen onto the ground, I was tapping the rest of the wall with the butt of the screwdriver, showing her how loose the plaster was. She was stood between me and the wall. We were really close – and she wasn't pulling away – so I slipped my hand around her waist and told her that, if she wanted, I'd be more than happy to have her right there and then."

"It turns out," Rupert continued, looking extremely downhearted, "that she wasn't quite as keen as I thought. She swung around, caught me on the side of my head with her fist, almost cracked me shin with a kick, and pushed me backwards. I bounced off the washing machine and into a huge puddle, soaking me strides in some brown gunk."

"But Boss. As I laid there, the clammy goo seeping into my trousers, I looked up at her and, through the fire in her eyes, I saw passion. She wanted me.

I knew it. She just hadn't realised it. Yet. But I'm sure, given the chance again, if I.............

Gazza had long stopped listening. He still had Rupert's phone in his hand and was flicking back through his picture library. This job looked like some really easy money. One that seemed too good to miss out on. And it would give him the perfect cover to get those appliances they'd dumped there sorted out.

Chapter 25

Gazza waited until Rupert had paused for breath while waxing lyrical about his new-found love. Jumping in before he had a chance to drone on any further, he told him to get her on the phone and tell her to meet us in the park at six the following morning. Rupert didn't need to be asked twice. Gazza watched the words *My Future Wife* appear on Rupert's phone screen as he pressed the name added to his list of Favourites only an hour earlier.

During a conversation that was over far more quickly than Rupert had hoped, Jean agreed, somewhat hesitantly, to the crack of dawn meeting and, following considerable discussion, considerably more reluctantly, to come armed with £1500 in cash.

At half past five the following morning, the streets of central Lancaster were almost totally devoid of traffic. And, as far as Gazza could see from the passenger seat window of the unmarked white van, even fewer pedestrians had bothered to make an appearance at such an unearthly hour. Dylan was at the wheel, with Dougal, Brian and Rupert in the back, making sure the slightly dodgy coupling connecting the van to the cement mixer it was towing remained attached. That task had been made slightly more challenging the moment Dylan decided to mount the curb, at speed, in order to take a short cut across the park. Still, they'd made it to Dennis's bench intact and, as far as Gazza could judge, without creating any outside interest or fuss.

By five forty-five, Gazza's offspring and Rupert had loaded the three fly-tipped kitchen appliances he'd been so worried about into the back of the van and moved the cement mixer into the dent in the ground where the washing machine had been resting. They'd also removed their balaclavas, donned earlier as they'd excitedly exited the back of the van, commando style (another one of Dylan's ideas), to conceal their identities while painting over the lenses of the CCTV cameras on top of the wall. Gazza felt that Rupert had done well spotting the devices peering down during his initial recce of the site. He'd have come across them quite soon after meeting Jean and would undoubtedly have been totally distracted and in full-on wooing mode. Anyway, as Rupert had said, quite rightly, "You never know who installed these things, nor what they were supposed to be pointing towards. Or, come to that, if they are even wired up to anything. Either way," he mused, "it's probably best to take them out of the equation."

Gazza mulled over Rupert's musings. Were these indeed long-forgotten devices put up many years ago by a person or persons unknown for purposes equally long since forgotten? Or perhaps a more recent police ploy designed to keep tabs on the local down and outs? Worse still, could they be part of the Council's current initiative to help combat illegal fly-tipping. Whatever the truth behind their existence, Gazza had agreed that these cameras needed to be dealt with before any work on the wall or clearing away the kitchenalia began. A few dollops from a 25 litre tin of thick, oil-based emerald green paint he'd picked up from a chap in the pub for a knockdown price only last week seemed as good a medium as any to thwart prying eyes. If there was anyone out there trying to keep tabs on what was going on, or, more importantly, who might be carrying out said goings on, this should scupper 'em.

With everything in place, Gazza and his four helpers were now stood around the mixer, waiting for Jean to arrive. The sun had yet to make an appearance, and with little or no help from the fading moon, they could barely see anything more than twenty odd yards away. But, as if on cue, as the church clock struck six, a slight figure appeared out of the gloom, striding towards them. The gormless look that had suddenly crossed Rupert's face, together with a heavy yet contented sigh, was enough to convince Gazza he was about to meet Jean.

Once the initial pleasantries had been dispensed with, Gazza took charge. He marshalled the troupes, distributed picks and shovels, fired up the cement mixer and set his merry band to work. Everything was going to plan. Constantly reminding his love struck aide to keep his mind on the job in hand was the only real managerial challenge he was faced with and, by two pm, Gazza was sat at the corner table in his favourite pub, The Stonewall Tap, sipping a pint of Pedigree and feeling pretty pleased with himself.

The wall along the remote edge of Ryelands Park was now no longer adorned with paint or spray of any kind, having been neatly plastered over. The fridge, dishwasher and washing machine that had been lying at its base these past few days had also disappeared, and his pockets were bugling with £1396.65: £1500 less the five twenty-pound notes he'd grudgingly given to Rupert and £3.35 he'd handed over with far greater enthusiasm to Dave behind the bar.

The only two things occupying his mind at that moment were how good the beer tasted and when it might be the best moment to call on one of Lancaster's renowned public servants.

Chapter 26

The following morning, Gazza strode confidently up the path to number 5, Primary Avenue and rang the bell.

There was no reply.

Peering through the opaque glass in the centre of the door, he could see nothing to suggest there was any activity going on inside, and when his call through the letterbox was greeted with nothing other than silence, he walked back down the drive, got into his car and drove off.

When he returned later that day, he didn't bother getting out of the car. The house was in total darkness; not even the porch light was on. Unless the inhabitants were deliberately lying low and trying to avoid contact with the outside world, he was pretty sure there was still no one at home.

The next morning, Gazza was again unsuccessful in finding anyone to answer the door of this large, four-bedroom detached property in this desirable part of town. When he returned to the Avenue eight or so hours later, there was plainly still no life inside number five. He was just about to drive off when a dark blue Mercedes swept past him, up the drive and coming to a stop close to the garage door. Gazza waited for the driver to finish collecting his things and get out of the car before joining him as the figure made his way to the front door. He called out, "Councillor Board. Could I have a word, please?".

Horace was, as he always tried to be when confronted by a likely resident (and voter), extremely polite. He gently explained that he had been away on business since Saturday and, having literally just returned home, this wasn't the most convenient of moments.

The Councillor's tone had been pleasant, although Gazza sensed a slight frosting the moment he said, "Actually, it's in relation to some building work I've recently done on the other side of your wall that I want to have a word with you about."

This piece of news seemed to cause Horace to miss the most modest of steps, although he was soon back into his stride, unlocking his front door and standing to one side as he shepherded his unexpected guest over the threshold. However, any thought Gazza had that Cllr Board was delighted to see him disappeared the moment Horace stopped him mid-way through unbuttoning his coat. The Councillor looked him straight in the eyes and said, "No need to take that off. You won't be staying long. Do follow me through to the lounge, though."

Horace made his way into the living room ahead of his guest. By the time Gazza had entered the room, Horace was already seated in what looked to him like the owner's favourite old brown leather chair. "Take a seat." Horace instructed, nodding towards the sofa positioned at right angles to him. "Now. What's all this about?".

Gazza sat back and began his tale of being engaged to tidy up a section of the wall facing the park. Looking over Horace's shoulder and pointing out through the French doors, he said, "On the other side of your garden, it would seem. Anyway," he continued, "it was a task me and my associates carried out, with, dare I say, aplomb, on Sunday morning just gone. I don't know if you've had a chance to see it yet, but when you do, I think you'll agree we've done a fine piece of work. The graffiti nonsense that was spread all over it has been removed, the brickwork lovingly repaired and, where necessary, replaced."

Here, Gazza paused for a moment, during which time Horace filled the gap, saying, "This sounds all very public-spirited of you, but I'm not quite sure what it has to do with me."

Gazza made to explain. "You know when someone gives you change for something you've bought and you put it straight into your pocket without actually checking it? And you walk away, not really thinking too hard about the transaction that just took place. But subconsciously, you're mulling over the words that the person at the counter had said, like 'Four pounds fifty-seven pence change' as they handed you the cash. And now that you think about it further, the coins you're jangling in your hand don't seem to equate to the amount they said they'd given you. That something wasn't quite right?

"Well," Gazza kept the story going despite the lack of interest being shown from across the room. "After I'd followed Jean Happs...... the manager of the project," he explained in response to Horace's expression of non-comprehension, "....through the copse in the park and found myself standing at the foot of the wall looking up at the twelve Nativity-style figures and drawings that I was being asked to get rid of, I suddenly had that very feeling. Something just wasn't quite right. Whether it was what this Happs person was saying, or what someone had told her, or maybe paid her to say, at that moment I had no idea. I just knew, in my bones, that something about the scenario being laid before me was not exactly as it was being explained.

"And then I remembered something I'd stumbled across barely a few weeks before on the Lancaster Town Council web site. You see, I read the Council's minutes every month. Without fail. You never know what you can pick up from the reports. They help keep the odd, honest citizen aware of new initiatives and alert to what is going on in general. Now, more often than not, that's where my interest stops. But while I was standing in that cold corner of the park, thinking about the merits of this wee £1500 restoration job, I suddenly recalled how the minutes referenced you, some scribblings on your wall and how the Parks Department informed you to get on your bike and pay for having it cleaned off yourself."

He paused, looking to gauge Horace's reaction, but none was really forthcoming. The Councillor remained rooted in his chair, staring straight ahead and feigning neither concern nor, as far as Gazza could tell, interest.

"But then I thought, hold on a minute. Perhaps the issue raised here by our apparent spendthrift of a public servant is not quite all it seems. What if he isn't bothered about trying to avoid the cost of cleaning all the mess on his wall at all? Maybe his real interest is getting ownership of this.... *mess,*" Gazza emphasised the word and paused for as much dramatic effect as he could muster, "....clarified and on the record, front and centre. Could his real motive be little more than to pre-empt any future question of who the wall and all things therein or thereon belonged to? Did he just want to make things crystal clear that the answer to any such question was Councillor Horace Board?"

Gazza continued, "The CCTV cameras were an immediate give away that something wasn't kosher. But still, I might have left things there had I not then recalled one of my boys coming home from his bar job a few nights before with tales of drunken insurance workers splashing out their bonuses on a huge policy sale to a local Councillor. Mix all this together with the dozen painted blocks on the wall I'm staring at and suddenly, four plus four plus four is very much adding up to twelve. Twelve very interesting days of a very interesting Christmas scene."

At this juncture, Horace held up his hand and said, "OK. Stop right there. I think I've had enough of this." He eased his way out of the comfy chair and stood facing directly towards Gazza. "This has all been an extraordinarily interesting account of what you clearly feel is drama and intrigue that strikes at the heart of Lancaster Council. But to be honest, I don't have the faintest idea what you're talking about. I have no knowledge of this Miss Hips, or Happs, or whatever the name of your clandestine moll about whom you speak and who seems so central to your tale. I am devastated to hear of the demolition of my mural, which, although I only owned it for a short period of time, I had grown to love. So much so, in fact, that I even paid to have it insured. And, if all that isn't sufficient to ward off any additional conspiracy theories you may be harbouring, I have been away on business since Saturday afternoon, during which time you say you were hard at work destroying my property!" Horace paused at this point. He seemed to realise that his voice had risen a notch or two and so, turned slightly away from his guest, took a deep breath and made calming motions with his hands.

His composure restored, he turned back and looked Gazza straight in the eye. "In any event. Let's just say for a moment that your ridiculous tale of *daring do*, intrigue and fraud is all true. You've said yourself that you've destroyed the apparent item around which my so-called little scam is centred. You've got no concrete, excuse the pun, evidence left on which to hang any of these wild accusations. So," said Horace, his emotions now back under complete control, "I think we've reached the end of this little escapade. I trust you've got whatever it is you were hoping to get out of this conversation, not that I can immediately work out for the life of me what that might be. And unless you have any other wild hypotheses or tantalising snippets of gossip or information you want to share with me............" Horace motioned towards the door, but Gazza was in no mood to leave. Instead, he stood up, took his phone out of his pocket and said, "Well, I don't know about gossip, but I think there might just be a chance you'll be interested in this because, you see, I kept a bit back."

He turned the screen towards the Councillor. Horace adjusted his glasses and found himself staring at the picture of a one-metre square slab onto which some yellow cartoon characters and a number four had been painted. It was propped up against the foot of a wall. Gazza started swishing through the pictures Rupert had shown him three days earlier, showing Horace the slab from a range of different angles. "I'm going out on a limb here," Gazza said, staring at Horace's face that was in turn staring, open mouth at his phone, "but, my guess is that, when you claim some insurance money – and I think we all know that's exactly what is going on here - for something that's been destroyed, your insurers might become a tad suspicious of said claim the moment a bit of the said item starts turning up in pristine condition. Examinations: many examinations will be carried out. Questions will be asked. Many many questions will be asked. Of course, I may be wrong. That's only my gut feeling. What do you think?"

To be honest, it would have been quite difficult at that moment for Horace to have told him, or anyone else for that matter, exactly what was going on in his head, beyond a surge of total panic.

Horace knew that the success of his little plan rested on the mural being destroyed to avoid there being any post-claim forensic testing. It was one thing for Paul Gunningham to say his work was as indistinguishable from Banksy's as it was possible to be, but he'd rather not have that assertion put to the test against some very physical evidence, thank you very much. The last thing he wanted was an authenticity debate with any one of Messers Gill, Wills, James, Farr, or, for that matter, Andrews, which might jeopardise his £5,000,000.

Horace slumped back into his chair. "What happens now?" he said.

Chapter 27

Gazza returned his phone to his pocket and started to resume his seat, pausing momentarily to plump up the cushion he'd left resting against the arm of the sofa. He squished it into place beneath his arm as he sat down.

"Well, let's see." he said. "Your £5 million claim for the loss of twelve pieces of art would come out at just over £400K a block. Now, some people might just switch off the calculator there and leave that figure as their fee for the return of a solitary piece. Or the price of peace between us, if you will." Gazza chuckled at his little joke.

"But that's some people. Not me. I'm a reasonable guy. I don't like to take advantage of another man just because, at that moment, he happens to be down and I happen to have the upper hand. I've lived through a number of situations where circumstances have changed and upper hands have suddenly become twisted around behind one's back. So, I've always taught my boys that when you're doing a deal, any sort of deal, it's important that both parties should come away happy."

Gazza paused here to give Horace a chance to take in what he was saying, not that the glazed look in Horace's eyes suggested he was actually taking in anything.

He continued, nevertheless, "Assessing you might not be over the moon at me asking you for a six-figure payment, let me suggest something a little less fierce. I propose a figure of around 10% of the slab's value to you as a fair price to pay. So, shall we say, £10,000, cash, and I'll give you the block back to do with as you please."

Now it wouldn't be fair to Horace to say that he just rolled over or took this all lying down. He blurted out fifteen reasons to the dozen why he shouldn't, couldn't, or simply wouldn't go along with such an outlandish proposal. "But this is blackmail!" was a phase to which he kept returning as Gazza calmly but firmly rebuffed Horace's objections one by one. Soon, his protestations were being spat out with less force and his objections with weaker justifications. In short, and within half an hour, the Councillor was beaten. He had slumped even deeper into his chair than before and Gazza waited for what he considered a suitable amount of time before saying, "Right then. Forgive the prose, but shall we arrange the exchange? Let me know when you can put the money together; used twenties, I think, and I'll deliver the artwork here – to your front door."

At this point, Horace seemed to rally and looked up. "Don't be ridiculous." he said, with, what Gazza thought under the circumstances was a tad more force and bravado than he'd expected. "You are not bringing anything up to my front door. Nor am I going anywhere near wherever it is you are calling your office. I demand some sort of neutral territory; I suggest we return to the scene of your grubby little scam and meet up, in the park, at the foot of the wall. I can have the money by tomorrow afternoon. Let's say five o'clock, by the bench. Now, if you don't mind," he said, nodding towards the hall, "I'd rather you didn't remain in my house for a moment longer."

Gazza tilted his head and parted his hands in an exaggerated form of compliance as he made his way out of the living room. Stepping onto the drive, he looked back over his shoulder and quietly said, "See you tomorrow. At five. By the bench."

"Don't you dare be late!" shouted Horace in an effort to have the last word as he slammed the door behind him.

Chapter 28

At 5 o'clock the following evening, Gazza was leaning against Dennis's bench, peering out into the park through the branches of the copse. The evening was cold, the night had drawn in and, as far as the gloom would allow him to check, there was not another human in sight. No dog walkers; no football kickers; no handholding lovers. But also, he thought, no Horace!

He'd arrived at the designated spot at four fifty-one, a time many would have felt was sufficiently early for a five o'clock meeting. Gazza, however, was not one of the many. Being here less than ten minutes early felt as bad as if he were twenty minutes late. He liked to be in control, to take things slow and to have the time to consider all eventualities. Turning up at a rendezvous at the eleventh hour was not conducive to such a regime. If a meeting was due to take place at 5 o'clock, Gazza would generally aim to be in position by four. Being ahead of the game meant everything and he would permit very few obstacles to hamper him. Alas, earlier, as he'd strode through the gate and into his yard to load the concrete slab into his unmarked white van, two such obstacles were about to present themselves. First of all, said van was nowhere to be seen. Secondly, and giving Gazza cause for a greater degree of anxiety, in the place where it would normally have been parked stood Dylan.

"What on earth are you doing here, Dylan?"

His son's reply of, "Living the dream, dad." didn't help, but that didn't matter. Gazza, breathing gently but deeply and through gritted teeth, whispered, "Dylan. What have you done with the van?" Dylan, looking up at his father and smiling like a puppy who thought his master couldn't possibly love him anymore, motioned to a spot at the far end of the yard behind the caravan. There stood the missing vehicle. Gazza knew it was his by the customised licence plate, G1 AZA, although beyond that element of self-indulgence, the truck was totally unrecognisable. It was now the most vibrant shade of green he'd ever seen. Head to toe. From the steel roof rack to the once, chrome door handles, to the metallic wheel hubs. Even the tyres had been painted a colour the Wizard of Oz would've been proud of. Dylan's explanation that he'd used the paint they'd bought off the bloke in the pub, "So there was no additional cost involved." didn't appear to ease the pain his father was exuding. Nor did he seem able to convince his dad of, he explained at length, the many benefits of camouflaging. But as he watched Gazza circle the van, twice, with his mouth open and his shoulders slumped, he grabbed hold of the fact that at least he wasn't ranting, raving, or shouting abuse at him. This, Dylan felt, was a good sign. Perhaps not the outpouring of love, praise, or admiration he'd hoped for, but in their absence, he'd settle for what appeared to be his father's tacit acceptance of the situation. This was, after all, an improvement on how his dad normally reacted to his attempts at pleasing him, so, given the circumstances, he was happy to quietly chalk this up as a win.

To a degree, Dylan had assessed the situation more or less correctly. However, although he was right that Gazza had not made a single detrimental utterance, that was more due to the fact that, at that precise moment, any and all words had totally failed him.

Resigned to the fact, as Gazza had done continuously over the years, that *being Dylan* was a trait in his son he just had to tolerate, Gazza simply sighed, "OK, lad. Come over here and help me get this slab in the back of the van". Nothing more, nothing less. Even Dylan saying, "Mind the paint work, dad. It's still a bit wet." failed to provoke further comment.

He motioned Dylan towards the shed around the back of the caravan, unlocked it and almost pushed his son inside. Just to the side of the door and resting against a metal cabinet was the slab with the quartet of yellow cartoon canaries Gazza had brought back, intact and in perfect condition, from the "demolition job" he'd been engaged to carry out those few days earlier. Grabbing a side each, they shuffled it across the yard, taking care and, at Dylan's continued insistence, not to touch any of his still tacky paintjob, loaded it into the back of what he announced should henceforth be known as *Gazza's Green Goddess*. His father said nothing. He simply shook his head and raised his eyes to the heavens, a double gesture he'd had cause to do in the presence of this son a thousand times before. Waving him away, he then slipped into the van and drove out through the gates, some thirty five minutes later than originally planned.

As he manoeuvred his way through the narrow streets of the town, he couldn't help but feel self-conscious. Well, he was in a dirty great big green truck, after all! However, maybe his luck was in (or maybe Dylan was right about the vagaries of camouflage) because he soon reached the edge of the park without, as far as he could tell, attracting any undue interest. Turning off the road, he arrived at the familiar stretch of parkland leading to the copse that was rapidly in danger of becoming a well-driven track. The temperature had dropped; it was getting late and there was hardly anyone about. A couple canoodling in an ageing Cortina parked up on the grass and a sole dog walker ambling away in the opposite direction from him were the only signs of life Gazza registered. He brought the truck to rest in a space concealed from the general public that, until recently, had been occupied by a washing machine, fridge freezer and dishwasher. It was 4:51 exactly. He climbed out of the van, positioned himself against the bench and waited for Horace to arrive.

After what seemed an age, he turned his wrist to check his watch. It was ten past five and while there was still no sign of the Councillor, he did spot some smudges of emerald on his fingertips.

He bent down and began to wipe the fresh green paint from his hands on the wet grass. He thought he heard something and froze. Not through fear; just to be able to hear better. Nothing. He wondered if Horace was toying with him. Well, two can play at that game. He stood up and called in a high-pitched sing song voice, "Councillor. Oh, Councillor."

Still nothing.

He tried again. "Councillor. Oh, Councillor. Come out, come out, wherever you are."

Suddenly, he heard a voice echo around the copse. "I'm up here, you stupid idiot. Hold your voice down. You'll wake the world and his husband if you keep that racket up."

Gazza looked up and saw Horace staring down at him from the other side of the wall. "What on earth are you doing up there?" he shouted, in as loud a whispered voice as he could manage. "And where's my money?"

Horace called down, "I'm not going to risk making direct contact with you out in the open. I've no idea what other ruffians you might have brought along with you. I have the money," he said, hoisting what looked to Gazza like a Lidl shopping bag on to the top of the wall, "but show me the piece first."

"I've got it here, next to the bench." He motioned towards it with his green hand. Despite arriving later than intended, Gazza had still had time to lug the slab out of the van and have it ready and waiting for the exchange.

"Bring it over. Where I can see it." Horace demanded.

Gazza 'rolled' it, corner to corner, away from Dennis and laid it on the ground flat and face up, directly beneath the Councillor. The four cartoon figures were now on their backs, staring directly into space. "How's that? Can you see it now?"

"Oh yes." said Horace. "I can see it perfectly. Just there will do very nicely."

"So that's our deal done then." strained Gazza. "Throw down the cash and we can both be on our way."

Horace lifted the carrier bag with his left hand and tossed it over the wall, to within a few yards of the blackmailer's reach. The moment he saw Gazza's attention had turned away from him and towards the cash, Horace decided this was the time to make his move. He lent his right shoulder against the marble mammoth he'd been resting against and, giving it as huge a shove as he could muster, dislodged it from its precariously cemented position, sending it crashing down onto the slab.

The noise it made was deafening and splinters of rubble were flying everywhere. Gazza stared down at the mass of broken concrete at his feet. Where only moments before had lain about eight percent of a Banksy, there now stood a large grey stone elephant, unblemished, plugged in its own pitch mark and staring him directly in the face. At its feet were hundreds, if not thousands, of pieces of mainly yellow fragments of plaster.

He looked up to Horace and cried, "What, for the love of Dylan was that all about? You could have killed me." He picked up the Lidl bag and looked inside. "And what's all this about?"

At this point, Horace seemed to become extremely agitated. "There he is." He screamed from the top of the wall and at the top of his voice. "There's the blackmailer. Get him. Stop him. Don't let him get away."

Now, anyone currently strolling through this section of the park who had been in the general vicinity about a week ago was about to see an identical scene play out in front of them. Two police officers appeared from nowhere, both brandishing torches and being lustily directed by a rather frantic Humpty Dumpty-looking character hollering down from the wall above.

"There he is! There he is! That's him! Grab him!" shouted Horace from on high.

Chapter 29

Some fifteen minutes earlier, at four forty-nine, the occupants of a rather unremarkable Ford Cortina watched as Gazza's green van drove towards them.

Sargent Greig had decided PCs Andy Trubshaw and Brian Turcat should take on this undercover job and they'd both been happy, nay ecstatic, for the chance of some overtime. The two coppers had met at aviation school where they dreamt of becoming pilots. Alas, it was only their dreams that were destined to make it to the clouds as both were colour blind; a condition completely ruling them out of any flying activity.

Instead, they decided to direct their enthusiasm towards serving their fellow woman and man in the police force; and the passion with which they threw themselves into this most public of service could never be doubted. Even the prospect of having to take the only available unmarked car, the dodgy old Ford on this assignment, wasn't enough to temper their excitement. However, modest panic had begun to set in the moment the two of them realised their quarry was hurtling towards them and about to pass within a few feet of where they'd parked up. Their helmets were already out of sight under a rug on the back seat and their uniforms were covered by plain blue overcoats. Nevertheless, they knew they were still two guys sitting in a car, in the middle of a park and looking to the world exactly what they were: a couple of bobbies out on surveillance. Trubshaw was the first to act. Without warning, he lurched across the seat, grabbing the totally unsuspecting Brian and forcing him into a fierce and passionate embrace. By the time Turcat had had a chance to react with a series of expletives and the threat of inflicting some serious damage on his partner's nether regions with his truncheon, the van had passed.

While Andy's quick thinking had avoided them being caught out, it still took him several minutes to convince his partner that the only motive for the unbreakable bearhug was to distract attention away from what they were really doing there. Brian was convinced, eventually, although from that moment on, he would forever more look at his colleague somewhat differently.

Sargent Greig's earlier briefing had been clear. The ruckus in the copse a week ago had somehow not gone away. The arrest of the suspected street artist cum burglar had been a catch everyone was pretty satisfied with. Even the district Super' had foisted some praise on them from down on high. But now it seemed, another crime, with the potential of even more and, dare we hope, greater, if not grander plaudits, had manifested itself. Blackmail! "We don't get much blackmail in these here parts of Lancaster." the sergeant said with his inherent hint of an Aussie accent.

The *powers that be* had valued the artwork painted by the chappy they had in custody at millions of pounds. How they'd come to that conclusion, neither Brian or Andy, nor anybody else in the room, for that matter, could fathom. Nor, it seemed, could anyone work out who, why, or perhaps even more to the point, how the hell, someone could possibly steal it. "It's on a bloody wall. Over 12 square metres in size. You can't just stick that in your kangaroo pouch and jump out of sight." teased one police officer at the back of the briefing, quipping her way out of Greig's consideration for the overtime gig.

The sergeant admitted that, while he didn't know all the answers, the information had come from a respected source. Greig announced to the eager faces looking up at him, "Councillor Board, the City Council's Chair of its Finance Committee and the owner of the artwork in question has given us the heads up. He's told us the thieves, or vandals, or," he said, slipping into the vernacular, "whatever it is these *Bruce's* are, have contacted him and made a ransom demand for its return. So. We're going to set a trap, lay in wait, catch them in the act of demanding money with menaces and – hopefully – get to the bottom of what all this is about." He paused before adding, "And if we need to start searching in any strange or unpleasant places for anything," he said, looking across at Constable Joker, "I know just where to come."

Turning to two of his more trusted troupers, "Trubshaw. Turcat. You were on this case last time. Take flight. Sorry, lads. Didn't mean to say that. Anyway, take the Cortina, get down to the park and bring me back some villains."

Chapter 30

The two undercover officers each had hold of a hearty chunk of their totally startled and nonplussed prey. "What's it......who are......how come I'm......" was as much sense as Gazza could make as he was being frog marched away from the scene.

Horace continued his yelling from on high.

"This is the man I told your superior about. He's the blackmailer. There. In his hand. That's the dummy bag of money Sergeant Greig fixed me up with. It's got all the marked notes. It's the evidence he said he'd need to secure the conviction."

The ranting continued, much as Brian and Andy recalled it had droned on the previous time they'd made the arrest on this very spot. Then, as now, they had long stopped listening as they *assisted* their protesting charge from the scene.

"He's the one who destroyed my beloved Banksy. My much beloved, £5,000,000 Banksy." continued Horace, regardless.

Sergeant Greig climbed up on the table next to Horace and watched as his officers led Gazza away. "So, where's the mural? I thought you said he was bringing it back."

"I honestly thought he was. And all of it, to boot. I was sure of it, what with the way he was talking and going on and on about the ransom." explained Horace. "I honestly thought we could go along with his wheeze and, with your help, had a real chance to get it all back. It turns out he just had this one piece he was trying to scam me with. And now, with me accidentally sending my marble elephant down on top of it, even that's gone. There's nothing left. It's all just a Christmas memory.

Greig clambered down from the table and began walking back towards Horace's house. He was mumbling something about having to get a shift on to catch up with Trubshaw and Turcat. "I want to get the marked notes logged in at the station before one of them loses the bag. It would be just like those two to carry out the perfect textbook arrest, only to mislay all the incriminating evidence before the formal charges can be brought. I think we also need to get the whole area where the bricks and stonework were destroyed covered and protected while we carry out further investigations. We don't want that wall contaminated any more than it already has been."

But Horace wasn't listening. He'd seen Gazza helped into the Ford Cortina and driven off out of the park; and now Sergeant Greig was out of sight too. He had a phone call to make. And £5,000,000 to claim. He wondered if Vicky would still have the sparkle in her eyes when he next saw her.

Chapter 31

Adam was back at the desk in the far windowless corner of the newsroom, staring at the cracked screen of the worst laptop in the office.

This time it had nothing to do with tardiness; he'd been the second to arrive that morning, hard on the editor's heels. But Ffion Griffiths was still fuming over his most recent missed deadline (Zoo loses meercat in cleaning mop incident) and had directed him straight past the empty chairs to what she now decided should forever more be the *seat of shame* against the wall.

While waiting for the computer to fire up, he drifted into his own thoughts, moping and reflecting on his sorry state in equal measure.

It seemed that only moments ago he'd been riding high, Sinatra style, Top of the list. Head of the Heap. King of Scoop. In fact, more than six months had passed since he'd first broken the story: *The Banksy, The Thief, Our Councillor, His Insurance girl* (the Star's sub editor, Pete Greenaway helped him out with the headline). And it had been a good twelve weeks since the trials.

His story of Gazza, *The Hands-on Handyman*, had truly captured the local imagination. As soon as news of the arrest had crept out, anyone and everyone was more than happy to provide Adam with wild allegations and recollections about their local friendly rogue. Putting together this story was the journalistic equivalent of shelling peas.

"His hands were always deep in many many pies." the baker had told him.

"He'd do anything for anyone, but you had to count your fingers after every time he shook your hand." was the local pawn shop owner's contribution.

"Did a very meticulous job on a house clearance once." an estate agent had commented. "I hadn't asked him to do it, but he was very thorough. I have to give him that."

Of course, some scraps of information tossed Adam's way were less useful than others. One resident, who lived up by the infirmary and made out she'd known the family well, had come to see him at *The Star's* offices. She'd made an appointment and everything. But the essence of her tale was that Gazza's son had once tried to sell her a share in the kiddies' round-a-bout in the market square. "He said it had magic powers, or some such nonsense. And then," she continued, "he took my lawn mower away and dumped it in the next-door neighbour's garden. I hadn't asked him to, but it served her right. I never did like her much. The mower was fairly new, though. Never saw it again."

The copy Adam had been able to generate on *Gazza and his clan* had filled the paper's front, back and middle pages with ease. And before long, he was feeding stories to the local radio station, which, in true local radio style, then went off and made up their own tales of dodgy dealings. Even *The Gazette*, which rarely strayed from publishing anything that people hadn't paid for inclusion, ran a few column inches of its own. All in all, the media was having a whale of a time and the local townsfolk were lapping it up.

Though not Gazza, of course.

He'd felt pretty confident immediately after his arrest of being able to blag his way out of things. He feigned total innocence as far as the Lidl bag of cash was concerned; and was sure the many fragments of smashed plaster could not be conclusively linked directly to him. However, with every day that passed, with every new headline that appeared, with every locally fabricated story that was broadcast on the radio, and with the publication of every new public opinion poll suggesting the people of Lancaster felt hanging was far too good for him, Gazza's shoulders dropped. And so did his levels of optimism.

Compounding his state of woe, the police began broadening their lines of inquiry. First, there were hints that the Banksy artist guy being held in a nearby cell had begun pointing an incriminating finger in Gazza's direction. What on earth might have prompted that he couldn't, for the life of him, figure out. He'd never even met the man. But then their questions started to focus on matters that Gazza knew would be a little harder to separate himself from. Fly-tipping and the disposal of numerous items of kitchen machinery started being aired in the interview room. Along with a few long-forgotten misdemeanours. There was the caution he'd received following an altercation with a snotty-nosed girl at B&Q over a Christmas tree being embedded into one of Snow White's dwarfs. The run in with the man whose house he'd cleared my mistake. (Dylan had been in charge of writing down the address). Even his son's unpaid loitering fines from hanging around the children's round-a-bout in the market square were thrown on the table. By themselves, they might have all seemed like small beer. But when lumped in on top of the blackmail charge, they just added to his pain and wore away at his resolve.

Of course, Sergeant Greig was an old hand at all this. He knew a beaten man when he saw one - and how to bring things to a swift and successful conclusion. "Look, mate." he said at the end of an interrogation session in his most gentle antipodean voice while putting an arm around Gazza's shoulders. "Blackmail. Wanton damage to a public servant's property. Causing pain, anguish and nightmares to a B&Q employee who thought you were being overzealous in admonishing a child. Ransacking the mayor's house. We've even got you driving a vehicle in an unregistered colour. Put all that together and we're looking at seven years. Five, if you're lucky. But come clean, son. Hold your hands up to it. Plead guilty. Do that and you'll be out in eighteen months. Two years tops. We'll even forget about the gnome. And we won't press any charges against Dylan."

At that precise moment, Gazza would have given everything he owned in exchange for the living Christmas tree he'd left behind at the DIY shop in order to 'donate' it to the policeman by his side. But when those initial mists had cleared, he sat focussing on the last eight words Sergeant Greig had spoken. He knew he'd been fairly and squarely boxed into a corner and after a few moments, he turned towards the kind Aussie face now barely inches from his own, sighed and said, "OK. I give in. Where do I sign? *Sport*".

While much of Adam's prose on Gazza had been written, checked, verified and published without any great journalistic difficulty, piecing together the personal story of Banksy, or Paul, or whatever his name was (the recent polls on *Beyond Radio* suggested the Lancaster Jury, consisting of just over 144,000 good and true, were seriously divided over the issue) proved somewhat more troublesome from the off. If truth be told, Adam had had to make up most of it himself. Forget invoking *Adam's Last Gasp Option*; this was *Option, Invent it all from the Very Beginning*!

Because, while Paul's path following his arrest would pretty much follow that of his fellow inmate, his tale was much more of a closed book. The only direct information Adam managed to come up with came from one of Ffion's contacts in the prison service. (She may always seem frosty towards me, he thought, but fair dues to her, she doesn't let that get in the way of progressing a good story).

According to Warden Gossip, from the moment Paul was taken into custody, he just sat quietly in the corner of his cell, refusing to say anything. "The police couldn't even get a 'No comment' out of him! He refused to see anyone. Refused a solicitor. Even turned away the chance of watching Stephen Mangan's Christmas special, *Artist of the Year* on Sky Arts."

And much to Adam's disappointment, despite numerous requests for an interview, he was equally unsuccessful in his attempts to alter the prisoner's communication levels or self-imposed isolation.

However. There was a wise and experienced head on Sergeant Greig's shoulders and, following his conversation with Mr Gazza, he knew when the time was right to strike and direct his good old Aussie loco parentis guidance into Paul's ear.

Ffion's informant was in on the interview and told her the prisoner listened to Greig in silence without putting up even the most modest of fights. "I doubt he was really listening when the Sarge put his arm around Paul's slim shoulders, spelled out the charges he was facing and how bleak not pleading *guilty* might really be."

"I mean, Mate." Greig had said to him, all quiet like. "When we arrested you in the park, you were in possession of one large leather bag." At this point, the sergeant moved in even closer to Paul, gave him a wry smile and, with a sort of knowing nod of his head, said, "That bag contained all the stuff reportedly stolen from the houses on Primary Avenue. Now, I know the handle had wrapped itself around your foot, Cobber, but that's still what we in the trade call *red-handed*."

"Anyway," the editor's snout concluded, "by the time we'd left the room and returned the poor wretch to his cell, he'd coughed and agreed to put his fate in the judge's hands. '*Whatever*' was the first and only word I heard him say during the entire time. Sure, it was odd, but I suppose it made writing up the report and sending it off to the PPS a lot more straightforward for the police than it would otherwise have been."

When news of Paul's admission of guilt came through, Adam thought this might just be his opportunity. Surly he would break silence now. And if he was quick off the mark, he'd have a jump on the guys from *The Gazette*. Maybe even a stride ahead of that painful reporter from *Beyond Radio* with the particularly annoying catch phrase, I'm Terri with an "I. An eye on you!" Yuck!

Adam's disappointment, however was to continue. After making his guilty plea, Paul was held on remand in Stafford Prison where he maintained his silence and his isolation. There wasn't even the chance of a photograph at the sentencing, as he had refused to attend either in person or via video link. Adam's sole solace was that this non-appearance also scuppered the person who, for some bizarre reason, is allowed to take pencils, crayons and presumably an easel into the courtroom to watch the proceedings in person, but heaven forbid the public at large should be afforded anything beyond a dodgily sketched pastel drawing of the accused.

On the charges of breaking and entering, burglary and wilful damage to private property, Paul was sent down for 2 years.

Due to a lack of verified information, the *facts* in Adam's copy had been sketchier than a courtroom artist's work, but his largely fabricated copy nevertheless made great reading, which was, after all, the name of the newspaper game.

His accounts of Gazza and Paul's stories had resulted in *The Star's* circulation reaching stratospheric levels, almost as high as Adam's personal stock had risen with *Jolly Jenkins* (as he made sure never to call her to her face).

Maintaining reader interest – which was also the name of the newspaper game - would be a challenge, but one Adam was sure he'd was up to.

His plan was to *reveal all* of what he described as the third part of this northern tale of intrigue: *The truth behind Lancaster's very own Banksy – and how it was insured for five million pounds!* All he had to do was find out what that truth behind it all was.

His first task was to delve into the background he'd need to produce a gripping piece on the financial element of this Lancaster story.

Adam had gotten in touch with every one of his usual suspects – and a fair few of Ffion's too. Alas, no one had anything at all to say about the way, or indeed why, Gill, Wills, James, Farr & Andrews had become involved in the matter. There seemed to be a total lack of interest or knowledge in how a park wall might one night suddenly be covered with graffiti and the next it be insured for £5 million. And not even a hint of fascination over whether such an amount had actually left the insurance company's coffers or, indeed, to whom it might have been transferred.

Adam knew his readers would lap up every word he might write on the answers to these conundrums, but first, he felt the need to stimulate their interest; make them realise these were things they really were desperate to know. In such circumstances, a journalist usually has two options, and fabrication is the often the default position they land on. It's certainly the easiest way to produce a few thousand words of gripping newspaper copy. However, he'd already played fast and loose with honesty and accuracy once on this story, in his writings about Paul. And he doubted going down that road again would prove convincing. There are too many trips and pitfalls for a hack to stumble over and into where large amounts of cash money are concerned. No, he'd have to go down that road, that dreaded track towards which no journalist who thinks she or he is worth their salt ever likes to turn.

Despite the shivers the idea had started to send down his spine, he knew this time he really did have to resort to digging around for, the truth.

Making an appointment to see Vicky Dunaway was a great deal more straightforward than Adam had anticipated. And when he arrived at the offices of Gill, Wills, James, Farr & Andrews, the chap at the reception desk couldn't have been more pleasant as he whisked him into one of their plush meeting rooms without even the remotest air of suspicion journalists often encounter.

He sat down in the chair, obviously intended for the client and mulled over what might be his finest shot at an opening line. What was likely to get this woman onto his side and talking freely.

When the person he assumed was Vicky Dunaway breezed in, Adam was leaning back on his chair, its two front legs hovering just off the carpet.

He nearly fell over as she passed him.

The difficulty he'd been having trying to work out his best line of attack disappeared from his mind instantly. In fact, the only line that came into his head was, *nice fringe*.

By the time she'd taken her seat on the other side of the conference room table, he had composed himself, meaning he'd managed to get all four legs of his chair firmly on the ground rather than ending up on his back with his feet in the air.

And he needn't have worried about his opening line because before he'd had an opportunity to even consider making some sort of utterance, she had dived straight in.

"I'm so pleased you got in touch with me, Mr Nicola. I've been following your articles on this dreadful and, as far as my company is concerned, unfortunate business very closely, and I like your style. But while the story you've written so far has captured your readers' interest, I felt it was leaving a large section of the tale untold. And as I'm sure you know, Mr Nicola, give people a vacuum, and they will soon fill it up with whatever nonsense their imagination might create. I don't want people making up their own versions of events. The reputation of GWJF&A is too precious to risk on that. I want to make sure an accurate account is put into the public domain from the off. Is that what you're here to do, Mr Nicola? If not, I wouldn't want to waste your time. And I certainly have no intention of wasting mine."

Adam couldn't believe his luck. Over 99% of a hack's time is spent being rejected or told where to get off. Here he was sitting in front of the person at the centre of this aspect of his story, almost pleading with him to listen to her.

"Of course, Ms Dunaway. I've been on the case right from the very start. I plan to see it through to the end *and* to make sure it's told properly. I'm the writer you're looking for. And please, call me Adam."

Did he detect the hint of a blush? He wasn't so sure. But, as she leant forward, smiled and said, "And you must call me Vicky." he didn't really care.

He looked directly into her eyes, hoping for a glint or wink that suggested some further casual flirting might not be out of line. However, to his disappointment, her smile just faded away as quickly as it had arrived. Instead of any form of encouragement, she leaned back into the chair, brought the tips of her fingers together and began to give him verse and chapter on the events leading up to the present day.

She told him how the provincial firm of Robert and Jubbers Insurance Services, based in Shropshire and specialising in covering farming equipment, had fallen on hard times. And how a similar but much larger organisation in Wisconsin, *Gill, Wills, James, Farr & Andrews Inc.*, who tended after mainly agriculture businesses in Mid-West America, had come to their rescue.

First, there was a wave of relief washing over the employees of the English company. A big American firm was going to ride in on a white heifer and save the day. Then there was fear. Might, in fact, the big American firm ride in on a white heifer with the intention of trampling them all to within an inch of their lives. Then there was optimism. The big American firm told everyone that this would be not so much a takeover, more a merger, a coming together of equals. The concern returned when the name of the new company was announced.

To be fair, the Americans had done as they promised. They restyled the company in both of their images, taking part of their own name and fusing it together with some of the name of the ailing English firm. It was just that the Brits hadn't really anticipated that the stateside contributions would be *Gill, Wills, James, Farr & Andrews*, while the bit of their firm's name to be retained was *Insurance Services*.

When the staff queried this, Jack N Gill, Senior Vice President and the *G* in GWJF&A, told everyone, "It's best y'all know where y'all are standin' from the off. Y'all"

After a while, things settled down as everyone realised that another of the SVP's sayings, "It's my way, or the highway." was not an option anyone wanted to test in the current economic climate. And so, with any possibility of mutiny averted, the new UK arm of the business settled into an equally new mid-western swing of things.

"But then," Vicky said, "came a series of disasters. Brexit, COVID, Brexit, Bird flu, Brexit (I really can't emphasise the devastating effect Brexit has had on the farming sector), not to mention *wheat blite* in the Plain States, had all come at once and hit the insurance industry in general, and their business specifically, extremely hard. It came as no surprise to anyone," continued Vicky, "when the American bosses of the newly renamed business decided to act. And it soon became clear that their plans would be going some way beyond some simple and savage cost-cutting. No, they had a whole new plan, centred around bringing in some of the top professionals from the insurance world to really shake things up."

She paused for a moment before saying, "And I was the fresh face poached from the city to get some new business on the books and revitalise the UK end of the business."

Apparently, at around the same time, an equally new brush, Joan Mitchells, was having her nameplate screwed onto an office door in head office. She had come in as Vice President, Marketing, with, it seemed like a free hand to do whatever she needed to do to stop the firm's freefall. And it was soon apparent that she had taken the brief on *doing whatever you need to do*, at least one, if not several steps beyond literally.

To begin with, she took it upon herself to launch a dramatic, world-wide promotional campaign. It started out OK; lots of bland, meaningless stuff: *We're the insurer you can trust* and *Our friendly team is here to help; GWJF&A – the firm you can rely on* blah, blah, blah. But when that hardly got any media interest, even in downtown Madison, she went rogue.

Suddenly, we were the insurance company that *answered your call within three rings, or we'll give you a $25 voucher for Walmart*. No one had any idea where that brainwave had come from, but everyone knew it had resulted in us exploding the wage bill as we had to take on and train an extra two thousand far from qualified call handlers.

Then we became the John Lewis of the insurance world: *Never knowingly undersold*. We committed to refunding customers the difference if they found the same policy on sale anywhere else in the world for a lower price. Joan didn't even put a *within 28 days* limit on the offer. Every Dick, Harry and Tom soon got onto that one and within weeks we were returning premiums centre right and left but keeping the same liabilities.

But her coup de gráce was the slogan she touted around all the major TV networks: *Gill, Wills, James, Farr & Andrews. We settle 98.7% of all claims within two weeks.*

"Now", explained Vicky, "as wild as that may sound on the face of it, it is possible. Anything in the insurance world is possible. All you have to do in order to make this particular declaration come true is make sure you are 98.7% picky about the business you take on in the first place. If it's quality stuff, very little of it (approximately 1.3%, in fact) will fail. And for the very little quality stuff that does happen to result in a claim, you can easily and comfortably afford to settle it PDQ, within a fortnight.

Unfortunately, that wasn't the business plan the rest of us were working on. I'd been taken on to insure anything and everything. If it moved, GWJF&A would cover it. So, there I was, in line with instructions from Head Office, writing oodles of business. Some of it you'd describe as great. Some, perhaps of lower calibre, but still good. Some might generously be described as just about OK. Some, however, were bound to end up categorised as, shall we say, *dodgy Banksy murals*."

Adam chipped in and asked Vicky if she'd underwritten the painting in a fit of pique or perhaps over enthusiasm?

Vicky let the inferred criticism pass her by.

"I'll admit I was excited. Everyone in my team, in fact, the whole UK branch, was excited. This was potentially very rich pickings for us. So long as the item is genuine, you can make some serious money insuring it. And things like a Banksy are surprisingly straight-forward to authenticate. Also, they're not all that difficult to put a value on. *Girl with Balloon* sold for $1.4 million in 2018; and more recently, the hammer price for *Show Me the Monet* was $9.8 million."

"So how did you come up with a £5 million tag?" asked Adam.

"Well." sighed Vicky, taking the moment to lean back in her chair. "It's all a bit of a balancing act, really. *Balloon* and *Monet* are contemporary pieces of art. They are very traditional in style and therefore likely to be of much greater commercial value than, shall we say, something daubed on a park wall in Lancaster. On the other hand, of course, they were both barely a third of the size of our larger-than-life Christmas scene. All in all, I thought £5 million was about right. Some people might even have thought it was a tad conservative. Not that Horace was one of them. I later found out that it had taken all of his willpower not to whoop and scream with delight or kiss every last body in the room when he saw the figure written in the policy. Anyway, whether you consider the business I was writing great, good, OK, or dodgy, it was making the figures look super. But the moment any of the deals went sour and a claim was made, we had Madam Vice President's *guarantee* to live up to. We were forced to settle said claims in double quick time and with no chance to check things out. The theory or expectation was that said *things* had been checked out beforehand and therefore any claim must surely be kosher."

At this point, Adam felt Vicky had drifted off somewhere. Perhaps wrestling with the question of whether the American marketing whirlwind was entirely to blame for the five million pound dent in the UK branch's figures. Or might a reasonable slice of recrimination be justified in being directed her way. He let her dwell on her thoughts without comment and it wasn't long before her mind returned to the plush corner office meeting room.

"I said at the start of this meeting that I'd agreed to see you because I wanted to ensure the truth of this sorry tale is the one put into the public domain. That wasn't the only reason. Adam. I know there's something fishy with this whole Banksy thing. And this, Councillor Board chap. In fact, I'm convinced there's very little above board where he's concerned. But that's all I have. A feeling. A sense. A belief I've been *done over*. I've been made to look a fool and I won't stand for that. I'm determined to get to the bottom of just what has happened here – maybe even get the company's money back. So that's the other reason you're sitting here. I want an investigative journalist at the top of their game to help me. Well, Mr Nicola. Adam. Can you play at being a detective as well as a newspaperman?"

Adam looked her straight in the fringe. "Listen. You've given me enough to write your side of this three-cornered story. And I promise you that what I write will be sympathetic to the firm and as gentle as possible on you. You'll see. Call me once you've read it. If you think I haven't delivered on my promise, we'll leave it there. But if you like what I've written, then you'll come out with me and we'll discuss it over dinner. What do you say?"

Adam continued before she'd had a chance to decline his offer. "And as for me doing some investigative work, I was born to be a Private Eye. I'll start digging around straight away. And I guarantee, I will get to the bottom of whatever it is our precious little Horace has been up to."

He let that hang in the air before standing up and saying as he left the room, "Don't forget. Call me as soon as you've read my piece on you."

Adam went straight back to the office and started writing furiously. Everyone knew the tales of Gazza and Paul. He now dovetailed their stories into those of Councillor Board and the multimillion-pound insurance claim. He tried to spice things up, building in as much intrigue as he could muster about the workings of the insurance world, praising, as much as he dared, the English Miss Fringe's role, while pouring a damper on Madam Marketing's actions on the other side of the Atlantic. The finished article was greeted with, he classified it as, *wild acclaim* (Ffion quite liked it) and a surge in sales (Ffion really really liked that). The third part of the trilogy was complete. And yes. Adam had undoubtedly made his mark with the stories on Gazza, Paul, and Vicky.

However, marks can soon fade.

His old tutor at Cardiff Uni, Bradley Meaner, used to start every one of his journalism classes with the exact same words. "In the newspaper business, you are only as good as your last story." Adam had taken to rolling his eyes every time he heard the professor utter this dull sentence. "He's repeated it so often,"

Adam used to reflect, "he should be done for a crime, not a misdemeanour!" Anyway, now Mr Meaner's catch phrase had reared its head again.

It had been weeks since his scoops had become chip wrappers and ages since his name had last appeared above the fold. The laurels on which he'd been resting were well and truly faded and Ffion had been on his back to get some new ones to wear. He somehow had to get his mojo back but was at a total loss as to the right direction to set off in search of it.

His mind drifted away from possible stories towards that of Vicky's hairstyle. He remembered the last words he'd said to her. "Call me as soon as you've read my piece on you."

It had been some weeks since *The Star* had published *The truth behind the Banksy pay out*, but his phone hadn't once been triggered into displaying her name under *calls received*.

He wondered momentarily if she could possibly just be playing it cool, although he dismissed that idea as quickly as it came. There was absolutely no chance he could ever be that lucky. Maybe she required some prodding, he reasoned. Perhaps a gentle reminder of how good a catch was. He just needed to happen on the right line of attack.

There then followed five minutes of total daydreaming before Adam came to the conclusion that he would have to call her. His next three hundred-second reverie was spent trying to come up with an excuse for calling her.

Adam knew from experience that *cheesy* lines seldom worked. Unfortunately, Adam also knew *cheesy* was pretty much his default position. On the tenth or eleventh time he discounted variations of "What's a nice girl like you, etc etc...", he had a brainwave. Stick to what you know and what you are good at. I'll phone and tell her I'm making headway on Horacegate! He made a mental note to keep the exclamation mark and use it in all future articles. Terri with an I will spit tacks at not having thought of it first.

Of course, the problem with this cunning plan was that he hadn't actually made any progress on Horacegate! at all. He'd gone over and over his notes on everything he and everyone else had written on the subject, but he just couldn't find a fresh direction in which to turn.

But then it hit him. From that briefest of thoughts, Adam had conjured up his answer. It's not a brand new take on the same old answers that are required here. There were some brand new questions that needed to be asked.

The more he thought about it, the more Adam warmed to his wave of inspiration. If his hunch was right, he might get right to the heart; dare he even say the word, *truth* behind what has really happened in this corner of Lancashire over the past year. And almost by way of a bonus, he'd make Ffion happy with a brand new story line and have a real opportunity for a second chance at Vicky. Yes. If he played this correctly, Adam thought he might not only sort out Horace Board, he'd also net two birds. And with a single stone.

Chapter 32

Four totally frustrating weeks had passed since Adam had put Operation *Horacegate!* into action. He'd typed out two almost identical letters within half an hour of deciding on his plan and, enclosing stamped and self-addressed envelopes, mailed them on his way home from the office that very night (he didn't trust *The Star's* internal post system). Since that day, however, only bills and pizza delivery fliers had been popped through his mailbox. If truth be told, he'd really only anticipated one of his two missives to prompt a response; the other had been sent more in hope than expectation. However, massive frustration turned to total delight when, after a month of nothing much beyond cut-price deals on *quattro formaggi's*, he returned home to find not one but two envelopes, written in his own fair hand, lying on the mat.

The first one he opened was the reply he'd anticipated. He would have been personally disappointed, and his plan totally scuppered, if Gazza hadn't given the thumbs up to his request to visit him. On slitting open the envelope, Adam found no chatty; *it was nice to hear from you* note, just a single piece of paper, headed HMP Stafford and signed at the bottom by Ian West, Governor. In between had been written his name and the date he had been authorised to *call on Prisoner 190255, John Gascoigne Danot.*

He placed the visiting chit on his hall table, wedging it beneath the art deco-style bronze statue his parents had bought for him as a moving in present. Deciding, at least for the moment, not to ponder further on the discovery of Gazza's real name nor dwell on the fact he felt he'd just been invited to transport back to the 1800's and *call on* someone serving at His Majesty's pleasure, he picked up the second envelope. Holding two of the corners between his index fingers and flicking it over and over with alternate backward swipes of his middle digits, he willed that it contained an equally positive response.

As soon as Adam removed the slip of paper, he saw that his prayers had been answered. Whether it was just his lucky day or because Maximillian Kolbe is the patron saint of both prisoners and journalists, he knew not. But whatever the reason, his wish had been granted. He had been authorised to call on Prisoner 090256, Paul Gunningham.

Chapter 33

On closer inspection of the prison's communications, he saw that the Gods hadn't shone down on him without throwing in a modest amount of cloud cover because his two visits had been authorised for different days. Still, the train journey is direct to Stafford and takes less than an hour and a half; he'd just need to justify two lots of ticket expenses to Ffion rather than one.

Prisoner 090256 was to be first up the following Monday. Adam caught the first commuter train out of Lancaster, arriving in Stafford just a few moments late at 08:30. He was first off the train and out of the station, where he found a queue of taxis waiting on the rank. He jumped in the one at the head of the line, asked to be taken to the prison and settled back in the seat for the ride. However, sensing the tone of the driver when he replied that he hadn't "…..been waiting all effing morning on effing line for the last effing hour for an effing half-mile fare that won't even cause my effing metre to tick over once….", Adam sheepishly slid out of the cab, mumbling that, on reflection, perhaps he'd make the journey on foot. Punching the prison's details into Google Maps, he crossed the road and started making his way through Victoria Park, past Home Bargains, along Gaol Square and into Gaol Road. He was at the prison gates by 8:45, ninety minutes before his allotted time.

Ffion had turned all sweetness and light the moment she heard he'd secured a meeting with Gunningham. She not only approved his travel expenses but volunteered that the nearest Premier Inn was barely a couple of miles from the jail (he didn't query how she seemed to know that off the top of her head) and he should feel free to stop over there if the need arose. She also gave her Warden chum a call. As it happens, he was scheduled to be on duty that Monday and had agreed to help *fast-track* Adam through the vagaries of a prison visit. Perhaps the God's had changed their minds.

Ffion told Adam her contact's name was Brian. Brian Wardon. Adam said, "Blimey. Warden Wardon. You couldn't make it up, could you." From Ffion's blank expression, she clearly didn't have a clue what he was talking about. He drifted briefly onto the Monty Python joke of the chap who said his name was Mr SmoketooMuch, but never understood why everyone seemed to respond with, "Well, you better cut down a little then." Anyway, Adam decided not to go down that route. His boss had been way beyond helpful and he didn't want to do or say anything that might spoil that.

His early arrival at the prison coincided with Warden Warden's lunch break; the morning shift starts half an hour before the cells are unlocked and Brian had been on duty since 04:15. By 9:30, Adam's path through security had been cleared. To pass the time, he was sitting in the Warden's mess drinking a tepid cup of fairly weak tea and watching his contact plough, almost head first, into a plate load of sausage, eggs, chips and beans, all covered in what Adam estimated was half a bottle of ketchup. It was a tough watch and the conversation had been fairly one-sided.

Brian was clearly a man on a mission where his breakfast was concerned and given a choice of dialogue or a mouthful of food, the sausages were winning. He did, however, pause while buttering *another* slice of white bread to correct Adam on something he was saying.

"You're *not* the first person Paul Gunningham has seen since being arrested. There was a woman, apparently, who showed up the day after he was brought in. I wasn't on duty and so I only found out about it when I was processing your application for a visit. The rights of remand prisoners are different from those once you've been convicted and when this lass turned up at the gate, unannounced, holding some sort of letter from the Council relating to possible further charges for damaging park property, the Guvnor OK'd her entry there and then. Gunningham hasn't seen a soul since, but he certainly had a chat with that woman – whoever she was."

At 10:00 a.m., Brian had to get back on the landings and Adam was directed to the visitors' waiting area. Nearly two hours later, he was still waiting. Adam was beginning to get a sense of just how slowly time passes inside. Shortly after noon, he was shown into a small room with a plastic table onto which a brass ashtray was screwed and bolted. There were three non-matching chairs neatly tucked under the table, but before he'd had a chance to select a seat, Paul Gunningham and a female warden joined him. Paul slid back the chair furthest from the door and slumped down into it, dropping his shoulders and, with a sigh, placed both hands on the table. The officer took up a position leaning against the wall across from Paul. Adam moved the third chair, placing it directly between the two of them but facing the prisoner.

Adam was desperate to find out what on earth the meeting with the woman from the Council had been about, but his journalistic sense told him to hang back. All things come to the hack who waits, so he opened by thanking Paul for agreeing to see him and segued, quite beautifully he thought, onto the question as to why he hadn't agreed to meet him before now.

While he'd struggled to get Warden Wardon to drip-feed him information between forkfuls of beans, suddenly it was as if the floodgates had opened. For the next half hour, Adam barely got a word in edgeways.

Paul recounted, in minute detail, the moment he first met Horace Board, how they'd discussed him painting some sort of mural on the wall, the vision he had for depicting the twelve days of Christmas, and how he had nearly finished when the lights went on and the world went mad. He proceeded to explain how he was confronted by the police; the moment his foot got caught up in the handle of a case full of stolen goods; and how he looked up to see Horace leaning over the top of the wall screaming that he should be arrested.

"I thought it was all just some big mistake - that they'd nicked the wrong person. Like the time I was working for this publishing company: I was certain I'd signed J. K. Rowling. Turned out I'd got the *John Henry* of some geezer called J R Hartley. Similar initials, but that was about all? I just ended up with a whole load of yellow telephone directories and a pile of worthless fishing books."

Paul looked to Adam for a modicum of empathy, but the journalist was simply gazing back at him with a slight frown and his mouth gaping. He carried on regardless.

"I knew I hadn't done anything wrong. It weren't as if I was disrespecting public property; I'd had the owner's say so, for Christ's sake. 'Go and spray away to your heart's content' he'd said. I have no idea where them stolen stuff appeared from. And there's nothing to connect me to them...."

"........apart from your left foot." Adam chipped in.

"Well, I s'pose there is that." Paul accepted, "But I had nothing to do with any of it. I just kept thinking there was some sort of explanation for everything, including why the Councillor had seemingly turned from all but draping his arm around my shoulder, almost pleading with me to do some work for him, to suddenly trying to get me dragged off by the law.

It had all happened so fast. It was two in the morning and I remember still being sort of dazed when I was transferred from the back of the police van and into a holding cell. The night's events kept spinning around my head. How did this all happen? Indeed, what on earth was it that *had* happened? I didn't know which way to turn or what I should do. And then this woman from the Council turned up to see me."

So far, Adam had been hanging on every single word Paul had said, storing each one safely away until the time came for him to mix them all together into a story that would make Ffion's socks explode. But the introduction of a mysterious lady from Lancaster gripped his attention even more, as his instincts prompted him to pay even closer attention to the tale he was being told.

"It was late afternoon the following day. I was expecting a solicitor to somehow materialise in the way they always do on the TV cop shows. But the only person I'd seen all day was the bloke pushing some processed eggs and potatoes through the window of my cell door. I wasn't sure what the next thing I should do was when the food delivery screw said I had a visitor and should go with him. When we reached the interview room at the end of the corridor, he half pushed me through the door and said he'd be back in twenty minutes. Standing in the centre of the room, next to a Formica table that had seen better days, was a woman I'd never laid eyes on before."

Adam widened his own eyes and smiled, nodding his head in encouragement.

"She told me her name was Joanne Lead; she was from Lancaster City Council and she had a letter for me."

"A letter?" Adam blurted it out a little more quickly than he felt he should have. "Do you still have it?"

"Not anymore." Paul replied. "She burned it before she left. Said she had to. That, '....it was for the best, all round' apparently."

"Who was it from?" Adam couldn't help himself.

"The note she gave me was typed, in Harrington font, size 11, if I'm not mistaken, on an otherwise ordinary sheet of Basildon paper. One hundred and forty five grams. It wasn't signed as such, but there was a name at the foot of the page. *Horace.*"

Adam was slightly taken aback. Indeed, he was moved involuntarily, suddenly sitting bolt upright in his chair.

"Horace. Horace? Horace!" Adam blurted out three times. "What on earth did he want? Can you at least give me the gist of what he had to say?"

"Well," said Paul, looking somewhat more in control than the newspaper man sitting opposite him appeared to be. "I can do better than that; I can tell you *exactly* what he said. There is no painting I've seen or document I've read that I can't recall in total detail. Every brush stroke, scintilla, or comma. It's as if these things just get etched in my brain.

It was fairly short. And really, if I think about it, quite sweet. It ran,
My dear boy.

I had to write to you as soon as possible to tell you how deeply sorry I am that things turned out this way. I have your best interests at heart and can assure you that any thoughts you might have that I was involved in bringing about your situation are wrong. I can't, at this moment, explain exactly what happened last night, but I am already working to resolve everything in your favour. We cannot stop the police's investigation now that it's started, and you will eventually need to plead guilty. In the meantime, it is imperative that you see nobody and maintain total silence in the run-up to the preliminary trial. If you do that, I promise, I can ensure the case against you will be thrown out by the judge within minutes of the papers first being put before him. The wheels are already in motion. You just have to trust me. Say nothing. See no one. And all will be well.

Horace.

"All will be well?" Paul spat the words out across the table. "I spurned the offer of a solicitor and refused every request for a meeting, no matter where it came from. I breathed not so much as a word about what actually happened to anyone. I didn't even utter the phrase 'no comment' during the police interviews. I did everything he said in his letter. And then, on the date of my trial, when I walked up them stairs from the cells into the dock, the judge, far from tossing my case out, she threw the whole damn book at me. Two years. Two sodding years! And all because I met Councillor bloody Horace bloody Board. I'll give him *all will be well* the moment I get out of here."

Paul then just collapsed into sobs of despair. "I was too trusting. I always take people at face value. Always have. And I've been burned before. I just thought everything was going to be right in the end."

Adam didn't know what to say. After a minute or so's silence, he put his arm on Paul's shoulder and said, "There's nothing wrong with being trusting. It's a beautiful trait for some people to have. But you have to accept that life isn't a fairytale. If it's midnight and you're looking down and you've lost one of your shoes, it's not a signal you're about to be whisked off by a prince or princess; it's because you're pissed.

Paul looked up, gave Adam half a smile and wiped his eyes on one of his sleeves. "Like the time I got hammered in a bar just outside Bristol and when I woke up the next morning, I was in New Zealand on the set of The Hobbit dressed as an Orc?"

Adam said, not with any great conviction, that he supposed so, while giving as sympathetic a look as he could muster, but he was concentrating more on trying to make sense of the extraordinary tale he'd just heard. He had a hundred questions but doubted Paul would be able to answer any of them. He broke his silence, asking what he'd meant when he said Joanne Lead had burned the letter.

"Just that." Paul said. "When I'd got to the end and looked across the table at her, she asked me to read it again. I told her there was no need; that I'd gone through it once, which was more than enough for me. She shrugged her shoulders and, taking the letter from me, said, 'Well, OK. If you're sure.' and fishing out a lighter from her handbag, set the damn thing alight there and then. It was reduced to ash within seconds."

Adam's allocation time was nearing its end. As he stood up to leave, he did his best to convince Paul that he knew he was telling the truth. "I've got firsthand experience of Councillor Board. Sorry, bloody Councillor bloody Board. We'll figure out a way to get back at him, and with luck, maybe even before your time here is done."

He checked into the Premier Inn Ffion had pointed him towards, managing to sweet talk the receptionist into letting him check in a bit early without having to pay the usual £10 supplement. He made his way along the various corridors to his room for the night, fell on his bed and scrolled through his phone contacts until he'd landed on the general number for Lancaster Town Council.

His call was answered right away and he was put through to the Parks Department in an equally quick measure. Alas, it also took no time at all to discover Joanne Lead had left the Council's employ some time ago. There was no forwarding address, none that they would give him anyway, although the person fielding his call did say that one of Joanne's friends worked in another department and that she'd pass on his number to her if he'd like? "No promises, mind." she told him.

While a long way short of what he'd hoped for, he realised it was probably as good as he was going to get, so he ended the call and wandered down to the hotel's restaurant for an early supper. The fish and chips looked the least worst option and, placing his order with the same woman as had been on reception earlier – he thought, they really don't over resource in these places, do they - settled back in his seat. The food wasn't as disappointing as he'd expected, although he did spend the next hour pushing some rather hard peas around the plate and nursing his pint, all the while trying to make sense of the bizarre story he'd heard earlier that day. He finished his beer, paid the bill, and decided to slip back to his room to mull over what Prisoner 190255 might have to say about it all when he got to see him the next morning.

Chapter 34

Adam fronted up at the prison gates at 10:00. Warden Wardon had said he'd repeat the honours and fast track him through security clearance, "....and then you could join me for breakfast again."

The thought of sitting through another meal opposite the human garbage truck was not something Adam had any intention of rehearsing, so he'd arrived at what he prayed would still be early enough to be whisked through promptly for the visit, but too late to join Brian at his trough in the mess hall.

It seems his timing was spot on. The Duty Officer made no mention of his colleague. Instead, he simply flicked through some papers on his clipboard before nonchalantly buzzing Adam through the security gates. Nor was there a repetition of the two-hour wait he'd been forced to endure the day before, as, without so much as a break in his step, the guard escorted him straight through to the same room, with the plastic table, brass ashtray and non-matching chairs he'd sat in some 24 hours earlier.

When Gazza was escorted into the room, wearing the prison regulation grey flannel track suit bottoms and matching top, Adam was struck by the contrast between him and the identically dressed prisoner he'd spoken with the day before. While Paul had shuffled in morose and downbeat, prisoner Danot (Adam still had to stifle a snigger every time he thought of Gazza's surname) was focused and deliberate. Later that day, he was able to pinpoint the difference more specifically. While both talked earnestly about wanting revenge, only Gazza left him with the impression that he was actually determined to do something about it.

Of course, despite not having spoken to Gazza directly in the run-up to his trial, he was fully aware of his accusations and proclamations about the involvement of Horace Board in his predicament. Until now, those had been little more than the words of a wide boy verses those of a prominent Councillor. However, Paul's story yesterday seemed to pretty much confirm what Dell Boy

Danot had been saying all along. Now was the chance to get some meat put on that bone.

If there had been any worries in Adam's mind about how to get the man in front of him to talk, he should have feared not. If Paul's tale had come at a gush, Gazza spewed forth his story at a torrent of Dam Buster magnitude.

He started at the beginning with the strange phone call from Jean Happs. The game was up on his fly-tipping exploits, so there was no point in being coy about this retelling of events. So he wasn't.

"I smelled a rat right at the very beginning of this whole damn process. It was for the wrong reasons, of course – I thought this was all about the fridges and freezers we'd been depositing around town. The fact that it had nothing whatsoever to do with that shouldn't have made me let my guard down. I don't like coincidences, and the fact that I'm sat here dressed like I am in front of you is the reason why.

I thought I'd been clever, sending the boy, Rupert out on a recce. And when he came back with love in his eyes and details of an easy job with easy money, I really should have had my wits about me a little bit more."

Adam gestured that he wanted to throw in a question at this stage, but Gazza cut him off. He was in full flow and wasn't anywhere near ready to stem the tide.

"Of course, as soon as I went to Ryelands Park and saw for myself how the 12 slabs came away so easily in our hands, the thoughts of easy money staring me in the face must have barged any remnants of caution from my mind.

Keep the dozen blocks of stone to one side, I thought to myself. No point in smashing them up here. Not for the moment, anyway. I just had a feeling that keeping them safe and intact might not be the worst idea I've ever had. And, some days later, when one of my lads comes back from a night out in the local pub with tales of a group of drunken insurance staff mouthing off about their policy *sale of the century* covering the mural in Ryelands Park, I thought my instincts had been right."

For the second time in this monologue, Adam wanted to interject with a couple of hundred questions, but nothing short of a gag was going to stop Gazza's roll.

He continued with the story of how he confronted Horace at his home.

"He was all prim, proper and cocksure of himself, right up to the moment I showed him the photo with the block of canaries. Suddenly, he turned a shade of yellow brighter than the birds themselves. And it was at that point that I knew I was onto him. He looked broken and pretty much fessed up there and then. He effectively admitted the whole insurance scam right in front of me.

Adam sensed he wasn't quite being given the full picture about the meeting arranged in the park where Horace had agreed to pay Gazza ten thousand pounds, but decided, for the moment at least, to let that pass. He was keen to get on to what happened the following day when Mr Danot returned to the foot of the wall with the huge slab of canaries.

Gazza explained how Horace wasn't at the rendezvous as arranged; that he instead mysteriously appeared up on high, looking down on him from the other side of the wall. "And the next thing I knew, the slab laying at my feet had been smashed to smithereens by a bloody elephant!"

The narrator paused while he had what looked like a reflective moment of woe. Adam found himself drifting, wondering if he was forced to choose between delving deeper into the £10k blackmail tale or the introduction of a bouncing mammoth [woolly or otherwise], he'd probably follow up on the latter. That was surely the better option for a smart-arsed headline.

Gazza's voice snapped the journalist back to the prison interview room. "………and suddenly." He said, "I was surrounded by more cops than either the Sun Dance Kid or Butch Cassidy had come across in Bolivia.

Adam had a mental image of Prisoners 190255 and 090256, in their matching grey outfits, springing out of a South American hideaway, Gazza toting a bunch of Paul's paintbrushes in both hands and crying, "Come on, Horace! Is this the best you can do?" Behind them, on the barn wall, he could see four giant yellow cartoon characters, their huge heads grouped together and baring down on the scene, as if eager to learn how this desperate attempt at freedom would pan out.

Adam decided now was the time to try and get some of that meat on the bone he'd come here for. He looked across at Gazza. "You said all the slabs came off the wall pretty neatly, but I've only ever heard mention of one of them, number 4. I know the elephant put paid to that but, what about the other eleven?"

Gazza explained that they had indeed all come off the wall intact. "....nice and easy." And how he and Dylan had stacked them neatly away in his yard. He then paused for a moment before mumbling, rather sheepishly, "My plan was, first of all, to make the Councillor believe all but one of the blocks had been destroyed. Then, once I'd successfully squeezed some cash out of him in exchange for it, I thought I could come back, maybe once a month for a whole year and repeat the process with each of the other eleven Christmas offerings. It would be the greatest Yuletide gift I could possibly ever give myself."

Adam held up his hand. "But Horace gave evidence in court that you were blackmailing him for the whole mural and that you were supposed to have brought all twelve pieces to the park that evening."

"That was pretty cute of him." Gazza admitted. "It certainly stopped the police from looking in his direction for the missing blocks."

Adam butted in again, "But what happened to them? The police said they couldn't find any trace of them at your yard and accepted your story that they'd all been destroyed."

"Well." said Gazza. "In the end, that's sort of what happened. The first thought I had the moment I was arrested was that the blocks of stoneware lying under my caravan had, in the clink of a handcuff, transformed from my beautifully wrapped personal Christmas presents to horribly damning evidence. I obviously wanted to keep hold of them but couldn't risk them being found. In their absence, the police only had a million fragments of one slab. Anyway, there's nothing left of the Banksy now. I told Dylan just to get rid of the other 11 pieces."

"Any possibility Dylan didn't get rid of them." Adam half-asked.

"No, bless him. There's no chance of that, lad." said Gazza. "Dylan always does what I tell him. The moment I gave my son the order, it was as good as done. I said to him just get rid of them, straight away, and not to involve anyone else. Dylan always does what he's told to do. No. He'd have sorted everything on his way home from the nick before I'd had my first taste of prison food. He wouldn't even have mentioned it to Dougal or Brian."

Adam thought for a moment. "It's slightly ironic that when you were blackmai..." Adam changed tack mid word, "..when you were speaking with Horace at his house, trying to convince him that the whole of his *precious*

Banksy, bar the one slab, was no more, that the other eleven were in fact lying intact in your yard. But in the end, that's exactly how things turned out."

Gazza glared at Adam, making it clear that he was happy to be doing without such ironical whimsy. But the damning expression soon faded as he slipped into wistful mode. "If only we'd still had them. We could have at least exposed Horace's insurance scam, and I'd have been let off the hook."

Adam frowned, half turned away, but then said, "You may have something there. Horace was obviously happy to take it at face value when you told him that the only one of twelve blocks to survive your demolition job was the one with the cartoon canaries, wasn't he?"

Gazza nodded. "I suppose so" he said, although not quite following where the reporter was going with this.

Adam continued, "At the time, when you were sitting in his living room and turning his comfortable little insurance scam upside-down, he had other things on which to focus. In his subconscious, if not on every other possible level, it was easy for him to convince himself about what you were saying; that there was just the one remaining rogue slab he needed to worry about. Once his elephant had put paid to that and everything else started going his way, I doubt he'll have thought any more about it to this very day. Why should he?"

Gazza stared blankly in response.

"Think about it." Adam persisted. "What if we could somehow make him think back to that time. That maybe you didn't get rid of the other eleven blocks at all; that you'd kept them safe somewhere. That when you were talking to him in his front room, you were just giving him a line. Greasing him up. All the time planning to come back to him, time and again................" Adam stopped short of saying, *as you had fully intended to do* and just let the thought hang in the air.

Adam watched as an expression of realisation began to wash over Gazza's face. "I suppose it doesn't stretch the imagination too far to accept that I *might not* have been telling Horace the truth about the rest of the picture. But ...."

Adam held up his hand again, cutting short any further musings the prisoner was about to offer and said, "I really think we might just be on to something here, Mr Danot." Adam noticed Gazza's eyebrows jump what seemed like a couple of inches at this, the first formal mention of his name, but continued as if he hadn't noticed. "If we really could convince the conniving

Councillor that the missing eleven days of Christmas still existed, who knows what might happen. I don't want to get your hopes up too much, but dare I say, I think I have the beginnings of a plan forming."

Adam spent the final half hour of his allotted visiting time expanding on and developing the plot that had started wandering around his brain. Gazza, now more up to speed than he'd been hitherto, kept throwing in suggestions and ideas. By the time the guard signalled that their session had come to an end, they had a firm plan in place. "First stop is to go and see Dylan." was Gazza's parting comment as he was led away back down the corridor towards the cells.

Which is exactly what Adam intended to do.

Chapter 35

First thing the following morning, Adam set about meeting up with Dylan. Gazza had told him there was no point trying to ring him: "If he's lost one mobile, he's misplaced a hundred. Ring his number and you'll be on the phone for days speaking with the myriad of people who, over the years, have benefited from his carelessness." Instead, he followed the prisoner's *cast iron guaranteed-not-fail* instructions for locating his son in double quick time: wander down to the market square and check out the round-a-bout.

At 7:30 in the morning, not even the attraction's operators were about. But, as his father had predicted, Dylan could be seen moving glacially among the animal rides. Adam watched him pause to stroke the neck of the horse. Then drift on to pat the shell of the snail. His casual movements stopped on reaching the rabbit. He bent down and seemed to be whispering something in the painted steel ears of what was plainly supposed to be a buck. He might even have kissed the bit between its eyes. He looked up, snapping out of an apparent love haze, as Adam approached. "Hi, there, Dylan. What are you doing there?"

"Living the dream." said Dylan. "Can I help you? Do you want a ride on the horse. I love the horse. The horse is best."

Adam held up his hands and said, "No. Not right now. Maybe another time." He told Dylan he was a reporter for the local paper and he'd come straight to him having spoken with his father in prison yesterday. They walked across the street to the café that was just opening in anticipation of some early morning workers. He baulked at Dylan's request for a carrot and chocolate milkshake, but when he saw the waitress write down, *1 x Dylan Special*, assumed that he'd been in this establishment before, so let it pass. He ordered a coffee for himself and, disappointed not to even get so much as a snigger from the server when he added, "sans daucus," steered Danot junior towards a table away from the door. He spent a little time explaining the background he'd covered with Gazza the previous day, but moved on as quickly as he felt he could to the reason for the meeting.

"I know your dad told you to get rid of the slabs – which I assume you did?" Adam watched as a dopey look washed over Dylan's face. Taking a slurp of milkshake, he nodded. "Got rid of the slabs." I followed dad's orders. I got rid of them! "Just like dad said I should. Got rid of the slabs."

"Pity." said Adam. "But never mind. Your old man and I have a cunning plan. We know Horace believes the slabs are gone, out of the equation. That without any hard evidence, his insurance scam is unlikely to be rumbled and he can remain in the clear. But we thought, what if we could make the Councillor question what he thinks he knows to be true? Somehow give him cause to wonder if they really were destroyed, as your father told him the night he met up with him in his house.

Your dad thinks that if we can convince Horace the mural still exists – even only eleven twelfths of it – he'll do anything he can to stop that information from getting out and make sure the slabs themselves never see the light of day again. If we do this convincingly, we might just get him to trip himself up, make a mistake. Then we can have a go at clearing your father's name. What do you think?"

Dylan's face lit up. "We could call it Plan Gazza." Dylan mistook Adam's expression of total disbelief for one that just required a modest amount of clarification. "No." he said. "I know what you're thinking. But don't worry. If we spell plan with two N's, people wouldn't understand what we're talking about."

While Dylan was smiling and gently nodding, Adam began shaking his head in despair. Even putting aside the enthusiasm Dylan had suddenly brought to the party, Adam was silently admitting to himself that, every time he rehearsed *Plan Gazza*, irrespective of the number of N's it contained, he felt a little bit less convinced about its chances of success.

Dylan had stopped talking and was staring out of the window towards the round-a-bout. Adam was wandering down which strange road their conversation was about to travel when he saw a flicker of light return to Gazza's son's eyes. "Rupert. I'll speak with Rupert." He said. "He loves Jean".

Adam waited for some form of elaboration, although none was forthcoming. Indeed, it soon became clear that Dylan had said pretty much all he was going to say on the subject. So, trying to make the very best of a rather dodgy job, he said, "OK, Dylan. Rupert loves Jean, eh? How do I meet these two love birds?"

Chapter 36

Leaving Dylan to sort out a rendezvous, Adam nipped home to shower and change. Feeling refreshed and, dare he admit it to himself, somewhat optimistic about the way his day might progress, he stopped by the office. His pigeonhole was crammed with memos from HR and Accounting relating to his recent trips, the majority of which he barely glanced at before throwing them into the wastepaper bin. By one o'clock, he was back at the café, sitting at the same table where only a few hours earlier he and Dylan had met. A brownish-reddish-coloured ring of milk from the base of Dylan's milkshake glass had obviously been successful in its quest to avoid being attacked by a damp cloth.

Doing his best to mop things up with one of the paper napkins rammed into a metal can on the table, he stared out across the square. There was no sign of Dylan, but a young couple passing by the rabbit ride on the round-a-bout seemed to be heading in his general direction.

Sure enough, they came into the café but paused to speak with another man sitting alone at a table closer to the door. The man shook his head. The couple looked up, scanned the room and, seeming to settle on Adam, came over to him. "Are you Adam. Adam the Hack?" asked Jean.

Adam sensed another of Dylan's labels at play, so he went along with it, telling them he was. "But where's Dylan?"

Rupert said, "He couldn't make it. He had other arrangements to deal with." Then, turning to his right and looking lovingly at the woman beside him, he said, "This is Jean."

Jean nodded at Adam, but, rolling her eyes, she turned straight back to her beau. Rupert persisted: "He *did* have stuff to do. Honestly" Jean gave him a modest smile and rested her hand gently on his leg. She turned back to Adam and explained, "Dylan doesn't really like me." She paused for a moment before adding, "Or rather, the fact of me. I think he feels hurt that, these days, Rupert wants to spend more time with me than him." She paused again and, looking at Adam with a greater degree of intensity, said, "I've never actually met him, you know. There's always been some excuse or other for him to avoid me." Turning back to Rupert, she said pointedly, "Just like this afternoon."

Adam decided it was probably best not to get involved in what looked like a lovers' tiff and instead signalled to the waitress that they would like some drinks. The woman behind the counter nodded, although instead of taking down an order, prepared three reddish brownie milkshakes, which she plonked down in front of them. Adam was about to challenge her as to why they'd been gifted these particular beverages, but noticed Rupert was already halfway through his drink, so he decided to let it pass. He had the fineries of *Plann Gazza* to worry about.

He was all too aware that everything relied on the couple in front of him going along with what he, Gazza and, he supposed now, Dylan, had in mind. He really wasn't sure what he might do if, for whatever reason, they didn't want to be involved. He needn't have worried. It took less than a minute to realise there was no cause for alarm.

"That bastard," Jean started in response to Adam after he'd outlined his little scheme, "That bastard," she repeated, "still owes me money. Seven hundred and fifty quid! And he took me for a fool. Played me like a fifty pence fiddle."

Adam wasn't completely sure either what a fifty-pence fiddle was, nor what the difficulty of playing one might be. However, as he outlined what he had in mind, it was clear she was totally happy to go along with whatever it was that needed to be done.

Jean was considering the difficulties they needed to address.

"So the plan," she said, and looking across at Rupert, "*Plann Gazza*," Rupert smiled and nodded at this homage to his friend's contribution to the plot, "is to first convince Horace the slabs still exist; make him fear that if they're tested and found not to be the genuine Banksy article, his little insurance fraud will unravel. Then get him to agree to pay us a shedload of money, or we'll hand them over to the police. And then we organise some sort of meeting where we'll give him back the slabs in exchange for him incriminating himself on tape. Is that about the long and short of it?"

Adam sucked some air in between his teeth. "I know, I know it does seem quite lame." He put on a mock American accent. 'Hey, Horace. Those slabs we told you and the police had been destroyed. Well, I've got them here in my back pocket! Oh, and by the way, would you mind speaking clearly into this recording devise and admitting your fraudulent scheme, please?"

Jean sniggered in agreement but offered what seemed like a modicum of optimism. "Horace is sure to be wary. Of course he is. But he's also bound to be curious. And that's the doubt we have to prey on. Just sow the seeds in his mind that the slabs are still around and, I'm positive, he'll feel compelled to do something about that. He won't be able to help himself. He knows if anyone were to truly examine the artwork, they'd discover they're fakes. And he just can't afford to take that risk. He'll want proof, of course. But if we can find some way to convince him they really are still intact, he'll be desperate to see them destroyed and we may get him to trip himself up before he realises it's all been a hoax."

For the first time all day, Adam allowed an air of positivity to creep in under his skin. "OK. So, I'll get in touch with our cunning Councillor and see if I can begin sowing the seeds. Meanwhile, is there really nothing in your dealings with him that could help us out?"

"In short," Jean replied, "no. I'm afraid not. Nothing I have links the Councillor directly to the mural. There's not even any proof he ever contacted me. There's nothing anywhere in stone, excuse the pun, about him offering to pay me to have the slabs removed from the wall. All our conversations were on a mobile number that's proved to be untraceable." Adam looked at her, about to chip in, but Jean cut him off. "Don't worry. I've tried ringing it a million times, to no avail. The only tangible thing I have from him is this."

Jean opened her bag and pulled out a red envelope. "This contained half the money that he was supposed to give me. It has my name written on the front, but it's in capitals and the letters seem to have been written using a ruler. But that, unfortunately is all. There are no other 'convenient' words such as, *this money was provided by Horace Board* scribbled anywhere on it." Jean grimaced, scratched the back of her neck, then appeared to have a lightbulb moment: "Maybe it has his fingerprints on it?"

It was Adam's turn to grimace. He doubted that might be a realistic avenue to explore. Jean sighed and said, as if in defeat, "Well. I'm afraid it's the best I can offer."

Rupert had finished his drink and was surreptitiously trying to sneak Jean's away from her. He'd polished off half of her *Dylan Special* when she slapped the table. Fearing the worst, he made to slide the glass back, but her attention was elsewhere. "If we're going to trip Horace up into incriminating himself, we need to get him out into the open. Somewhere we can make him think he's truly going to see the missing slabs."

Adam picked up the thought and chipped in, "Not only find a place where he can see them. We'll persuade him that this will be somewhere the slabs can be destroyed once and for all. And all in front of his eyes."

He paused for a moment before adding, "He'll want somewhere quiet, hidden, but in the open so he can't be trapped. Is it too tacky to suggest meeting up in the park, back at the *scene of his crime*? It would be perfect for us, but would he go for it?"

"Only one way to find out." said Jean. I think it's time for you to make your house call on our local Councillor."

Chapter 37

The next day, Adam walked across town towards the park and into Primary Avenue. A dark blue Mercedes was parked on the driveway of number 5. It took a few moments for Horace to answer the doorbell, but on doing so, it was clear he recognised Adam immediately. Good, Adam thought. At least that will save on lengthy introductions.

"Good morning, young man. And to what do I owe the pleasure of a house call by Lancaster's premier intrepid reporter?" Adam felt the Councillor must be feeling either quite chipper, or particularly sarcastic this morning.

"I wonder if I might come in and have a word with you, Councillor Board. There have been some developments in the case of your missing Banksy that I was hoping you might comment on."

By the look on Horace's face, this was clearly the last thing he'd been expecting to be confronted with, but he soon regained his composure and motioned Adam into the house and along the hall to the sitting room.

Declining the offer of tea, coffee, or, indeed, anything stronger, Adam got straight to the point. "As you know, I've reported on this story for *The Star* from the moment the mural vanished to the arrest of the perpetrators. I probably know the ins and outs of the whole tale as well, if not better than anyone else. It's been a great story for the newspaper, and quite a profitable one too." He stopped short of saying, 'though, of course, not nearly as rewarding as it has been for you' and instead continued, "To be honest, I was sad when it all came to an end. But one moves on and looks forward to the next scoop. After all. It's been over six months since the sentences were handed down in court, and the insurance company paid you out......" He paused, looking for some response to this cheap jibe, but his host remained seated without any reaction, so he carried on, ".....and I'd pretty much closed the book on the whole escapade. And then, yesterday afternoon, a young man came into my office at the newspaper and told me the most extraordinary tale."

Adam leant forward in his seat, just a fraction, just enough to suggest that he had reached the key point in his narrative. "This chap, without preamble or small talk, and before he'd accepted my offer of a seat, stared at me square in the face and said, quite simply, 'I've got the Christmas Banksy. Are you interested in seeing it?"

Adam looked straight across at the Councillor. This time, he was prepared to wait before moving on. The silence was uncomfortable. In the end, it was Horace who broke. "He's got the Christmas Banksy? What on earth are you talking about? No one's got the Banksy. The Banksy is gone. I saw a bit of it smashed to smithereens before my own eyes. That Gazza person did for the rest of it. The police checked that all out and were totally satisfied. You've been had, Mr Nicola. A chancer. Someone who's no doubt approached you, hoping to get a bit of easy money from the local rag for some line or two that has no substance or worth. I'd have thought better of you, Adam." he said in as patronising a tone as he could muster. "That an experienced hack like you should fall for such a feeble lie. I don't suppose he showed them to you, did he?"

Adam felt he was in this deep; he might as well keep going. "Well, I've seen some photographs, which is enough to get me interested; prompt me to pop on my *Hack's* hat." Adam had been sorely tempted to add '*touché*' but decided not doing so was the better part of valour.

The expression on Horace's face suggested to Adam that he might be at least a tad interested as well. "Photographs? Photographs!" he blurted out. "What photographs? Show me. Where are they? Who took them? Where is this guy?" The bluster of questions was coming thick and fast.

Adam told him, "I don't have them. My source took them away with him." He paused, feeling that maybe a bit of empathy might not be the worst tack he could try. "Councillor. Like you, I'm suspicious too. For example, there was no indication when the photos he showed me were taken."

Horace's eyes widened. "Exactly!" He said with perhaps a little more emphasis than he'd intended. Appearing to regain some composure, he continued, "They probably are old snaps. Nothing worth troubling about, I'm sure." Adam sat back in his chair. "Well, Councillor, I'm not totally sure about that. As you say, it may all be nothing, but I'm a journalist. I need to follow where my leads take me. So, I have asked him for some hard evidence. To *show me the money*, so to speak. The proof."

Horace's manner had wandered into defensive. "OK. Where are these *supposed* slabs then?" he snapped.

"All I can tell you," Adam said, "is that they must be relatively close by and easily transportable, because he said he'd show them to me tomorrow afternoon. All eleven of them. On the other side of your wall." Adam nodded in the general direction of the Councillor's back garden. "You're correct about him wanting some money, by the way. Twenty thousand pounds for his troubles." Adam noticed Horace recoiled slightly at this piece of news, so leaning forward, he said in a conspiratorial tone, "I offered him five hundred quid; take it or leave it."

Horace also leant forward as if that would enable him to continue the clandestine nature of the conversation. "£500?" he whispered. Then slightly more boldly, "What did he say?"

"Well," said Adam, moving even closer to Horace so that their faces were almost touching. "He shrugged his shoulders and said he'd be in the park at four o'clock. Bring the monkey with you."

Horace looked puzzled for a moment, then said, "I presume that's some sort of gutter slang for that amount of money?" Adam nodded and said, "It's about twenty ponies, I think."

That wasn't as helpful a reply as Horace had hoped for, but he put it to one side. He was more interested in trying to gauge the level of truth behind the story he'd just been given. In the end, he said, "Well, if you ask me, I don't know about horses or primates; it sounds more like a wild goose chase. But I'd be interested in being in *on the kill,* so to speak, when the rogue turns up with nothing more than an empty van. I just hope he doesn't come armed with a knife or something equally sinister."

Adam grimaced, saying he hadn't thought for a moment about that possibility. Thanking the Councillor for sowing that sinister seed, he said, "Well, at least there will now be two of us. We can confront the issue together. Side by side. Shoulder to shoulder. Brothers in arms."

Adam breathed a sigh of relief as he left 5 Primary Avenue. Phase one of *Plann Gazza* was completed and Horace seemed to be on board. He just hoped his parting shot about *brothers in arms* hadn't over egged the pudding. "Ah, well," he said as he turned the corner. "I suppose we find that out tomorrow during Phase two."

Chapter 38

The next day, just after three thirty, Adam was sitting on Dennis's bench, hoping that Councillor Board had not had a change of heart and would shortly be making an appearance. Half an hour later, he watched Horace slowly cross the open ground towards the relatively quiet and concealed corner of Ryelands Park. Adam half rose and extended his hand, which was completely ignored.

"OK. Where's your man?" demanded Horace, walking straight past him and coming to a stop only on reaching the foot of the wall.

The whole area of wall where Paul worked his Christmas magic had been covered, literally put under wraps, by a huge tarpaulin placed there six months or more ago on the orders of Sargent Greig.

He'd wanted to get the whole area where the bricks and stonework were destroyed covered and protected while carrying out further investigations. His instructions to a couple of raw Police Community Support officers to "...make sure the bloody thing's secure. I don't want it coming loose and having to call out the red arrows to shoot down a runaway canvas sheet flying over the skies of Lancaster." had clearly and comprehensively been adhered to. Its continued presence was certainly a testament to that. Cuts in the police budget had caused the removal of the covering to fall way down the priority list; it would no doubt be taken away sometime, just not in the very immediate future.

The area that Tony Greig ordered to be covered was so high and wide that none of the usual materials at the police's disposal were big enough for the job. The brace of PCSOs who had only come out of training two days earlier and were at a loss as to exactly what to do had simply been told by their Aussie mentor to "....sort it out, mates". And sort it out they did, purloining (Sargent Greig didn't ask how) a large sheet of canvas from the fairground that had set up shop for the holidays. Its off-white colour had now faded to a dirty cream, but the red letters of *Big Kid Circus* at the top and centre of the tarpaulin remained as vivid as the day they'd been printed on. Some bright spark had spray painted on a door at ground level, giving the illusion of being able to gain access to, what would be, Horace's garden, where a Ring Master and several clowns might be waiting.

The Councillor stared directly into Adam's eyes. "So. Where is your mystery source? Where is my Banksy?" He made to turn away. "Mr Nicola. As I suspected, this seems to have been nothing short of a total waste of time."

Adam was feeling he couldn't agree more. Dylan should have been here to help field questions about the absence of slabs ages ago. There was only so much blustering he could carry on mustering before Horace would catch on that no paintings, or brick work of any form, for that matter, would be forthcoming. He was running out of phrases with which to stall. "He called me just before you arrived to say he's caught up in traffic." Adam's decision earlier to have his phone set to *record* in the hope of catching Horace incriminating himself was looking particularly optimistic.

Adam thought he'd start by getting the Councillor to at least admit that he knew Paul Gunningham.

Whether Horace suspected Adam might be up to something or if events had just led him to be constantly on the alert, it was hard to tell. Either way, the Councillor's demeanour could only at best be described as cagey. He said he had a vague memory he might have seen him at something organised by the local police many many months ago, but that he had no recollection of actually meeting the rogue. "Apparently it was some sort of event to help past offenders back onto the straight and narrow. "That was constabulary money well spent, I don't think!"

Adam then tried him with the widely spread story that he had conspired with Gunningham for him to create a fake Banksy on his wall. Horace seemed totally affronted.

"Before all this malarky," he said, waving his hand in the general direction of the wall, "I wouldn't have known a real Banksy if it had come to life and smacked me in the mouth!"

Adam finally went all in, challenging Horace directly that everything that had happened was all part of a cunning plan to defraud the insurance company out of £5 million.

The only response Horace gave to what he called a "wild and libellous accusation" was that perhaps he'd been watching too many Steve McQueen films.

Adam thought he may have hit a nerve on the suggestion Horace had robbed his own neighbours and planted the stolen goods on Paul, but the Councillor simply scoffed at such nonsense and pressed him about how much longer before the damn slabs were going to make an appearance.

Adam was slowly coming to the conclusion that his plan was getting nowhere. Once Dylan arrived – without the slabs – the ruse would be up. Without hard evidence, his bluff was destined to fail. Mere words and threats were not going to get through this politician's guard.

Horace must have sensed Adam's despair and, feeling emboldened, said, "If this was just some absurd ruse to try and trick me into saying something ridiculous or incriminating, it clearly hasn't worked. I'll be having a strong word with your editor and the proprietor of your local rag. You'll rue the day you started making baseless accusations about me."

Adam had the feeling this was just the beginning of a long rant Horace was about to embark on when Jean and Rupert appeared through the bushes. Horace was clearly stunned at Jean's arrival on the scene but somehow managed to keep things together. At least, Adam thought, it's taken his focus away from me for a moment.

"Good afternoon, Councillor," says Jean. "Nice to see you, *again*." Horace didn't turn a hair, nor did he do anything that suggested he had ever seen the woman addressing him before. Despite the snub, Jean continued, "If Mr Nicola hasn't managed to get the truth out of you, I'm here to tell anyone who wants to listen that you offered to pay me £1500 to get the Banksy destroyed. Why would you do that if it wasn't to fraudulently grab the insurance payout? I'm the living connection between you and your lies."

Horace turned towards Adam. "Who is this woman? I've neither seen her before, nor do I have the faintest idea what she's talking about." Turning back to Jean, he challenged, "Where's your proof of any of this? Where's the evidence I promised to pay you £1500? It's all just words. You don't have any direct links to me. No one has any proof I ever offered you money to destroy the Banksy.

At that moment, Dylan appeared through the copse and, in a somewhat dramatic style, gently nudged his way between Jean and Rupert. His entrance was slightly marred by half tripping over a tree root and almost falling into Horace's arms, but he managed to regain at least some of his composure and, staring directly into the Councillor's eyes, announced, "That, I'm afraid, is where you're wrong. Someone does have proof that you offered Jean the money. Me."

Horace, who seemed to be losing slices of his own composure with every new twist and turn the tale was taking, glared at Dylan and virtually shouted, "Who the hell are you? And what are you doing here?"

"Well," said Dylan, I'm living the dream. But as to who I am, I'm Dylan. But you can call me Bob. *B.C.H.* Bob can help."

"But you just said your name was Dylan!" squealed Horace.

"It is." replied Dylan. But some of my friends call me Bob. I'm not totally sure why, but I thought it sounded great, so I decided to use it as a *nom de plumb*."

Horace scrunched up his face and said, "Plumb?"

"No thanks." said Dylan. "I've already eaten. Anyway, my dad said I should sort out a little sideline for myself. Gain a bit of independence. So, I thought a new business, with a new secret name would be great. BCH. Bob can help. Anyway," he continued, "I'm the connection. I'm Bob. I was the one who gave your envelope containing the £1500 to Jean. Here's the picture you asked me to take of me handing it to her."

Horace was blustering. "So, you gave her an envelope." and then far from convincingly said, "Nothing to do with me."

Dylan waited a moment, then said, "But I've got other pictures as well. Earlier that day, while I was waiting to pick up the package from the PO Box, I was taking photos of people walking past. Here are four of them. You're in each one. And look. You're holding a red envelope. I've got another one where I've zoomed in on it. I've got this really neat app on the phone where it takes out all the surrounding stuff you don't want and brings some clarity to the...." Rupert gave a loud cough cum sneeze that sounded very much like he said, "too much info....". Dylan took the hint and returned to the enlarged snap. "Look. On the front. It says, JEAN. It's written very neatly. Almost as if it was done using a rule. And it's underlined."

Jean turned the envelope in her hand around so that Horace could see it. Sure enough, her name, written in capitals and underlined, was there for all to see. It was the same envelope.

Horace was still protesting his innocence. "All this proves nothing. For all anyone knows, it could just have been a Christmas card I was sending to someone called Jean. Maybe I dropped it on the road and maybe you picked it up while doing your David Bailey impersonation."

Horace snatched the photographs from Dylan's hand and stared at them for what seemed like ages. It was true that his eyes had widened. And his jaw had dropped for sure. But, in an effort to regain the high ground, his feet had begun doing some fancy tap dancing. "OK," he said. "Maybe I did offer this woman some money, but it was for some general tidying up I wanted doing around the wall. Yes. That's it. Once I'd found out this park side of the wall was my responsibility, I decided it was only right that I should do my civic duty. That was what I was paying her for. I didn't admit it just now, as I don't like to boast about my charitable exploits. Anyway, I certainly didn't pay her to destroy the picture. I had only known about it for a very short period of time, but I had already come to love it." The reporter watched in disbelief as the Councillor made to wipe away a non-existent tear.

"No." Horace had the floor and was carrying on relentlessly. "The only possible unanswered question relating to this whole sorry business is the authenticity of the Banksy itself. Now it would appear that Bob, or Dylan, or John, or Lennon, or whatever his damn name is, has not come armed with the remaining bits of the painting as promised. No surprise there." He said in as patronising a fashion as he could muster. "And as the picture no longer exists, there's no way of checking whether it is the genuine article. Or not. No evidence I have done anything wrong. At all. Without the slabs," Horace was now scanning the audience before him, addressing them all. "so heartlessly ripped away from my wall with your chisels and hammers," he said, emphasising the word, *ripped* while dramatically gesturing towards the wall with a sweep of his arm and stifling away a sniff, "you've got nothing on me."

"You're right." said Dylan. "Or at least you would be if the hammerers and chisellers had done their jobs properly. As it is............." Dylan stopped mid-sentence. He then turned to face Rupert, smiled the smile of someone totally besotted, and nodded.

Rupert had been ready and waiting for his moment in the sun to perform the one simple task he'd been given. And he wasn't going to muck it up. With a tug on the rope no one had realised he'd been holding all this time, the huge police tarpaulin covering the wall in which shadow everyone had been standing fell to the ground. Horace, attracted by the sound of the sheet crashing onto the hard earth, stood staring at the vast expanse of canvas now lying concertinaed by his feet. He was soon distracted, though, by the sound of applause. Jean and Dylan were clapping wildly, motioning towards Rupert, who was bowing as deeply and reverently as someone greeting the Japanese Emperor. As he returned to the upright position, he twisted his head away from his admirers and looked up towards the freshly revealed wall. Horace followed his stare.

Horace's jaw dropped further and his eyes widened more broadly than they ever had before. Towering above him, as if they had never been anywhere else since the day they were painted, were slabs numbered one to three and five to twelve. The area on the bottom right-hand corner of the wall where Day 4 should have been was empty. But the effect was none the less for it.

If this was something Horace was not expecting, it was, without doubt, the last thing Adam and Jean had anticipated. The three of them were clearly in a similar state of shock, all screaming and pointing upwards at the same time, "How did this get up here?"

Horace couldn't comprehend what was happening. His eyes switched from the incomplete Christmas scene to Dylan and then to Rupert, who was still proudly clinging to his rope. He looked back up at the wall. At the perfectly painted pictures. He seemed to be counting the blocks, adding them up as if he needed proof that all eleven of the pieces he had been convinced had been destroyed were indeed right in front of him. He then turned to face Adam, who had the air of a man just as dumbfounded as he was.

Adam was babbling. "What on..... who on.... where on earth has this come from?" Turning to Dylan and, in a slightly more controlled tone, said "You told me you'd destroyed it. Your father said as much. How did....? What was the....? Why is it ....."

Dylan must have felt the moment had come to put Adam out of what was obviously a very painful and disorienting misery. He started rather simply by saying, "No." Then, after a few moments, during which it became apparent, even to Dylan, that Adam needed a slightly more comprehensive explanation, continued, "Dad only asked me to get rid of it. He said nothing about destroying anything. I hid the slabs away in the base of the round-a-bout in the market square. It's magic, that round-a-bout." Dylan's eyes misted over. He was clearly in a very special, personal place.

On his return to the real world, he added, "Anyway, when you told me what you wanted to do, I thought that instead of trying to make the Councillor believe the Banksy hadn't been destroyed, why not just show him that it was still alive and kicking." Dylan screwed up his face, clearly wrestling with whether or not his metaphor had made sense. Deciding it probably did need at least a modest amount of clarification said, "However much a few lumps of stone can be kicking. Or, I suppose, alive."

The dramatic events that had just knocked Adam sideways had prompted him to conduct his own bout of internal wrestling. Not that Dylan's choice of prose was among the things he was finding it difficult coming to terms with.

The sound of Horace's voice put Adam's struggle to comprehend exactly what had just happened on hold. "But it's no good testing or getting an expert to look at this." The Councillor was in what could only be described as a high-pitched scream mode. "Young master Gunningham promised me it was almost impossible to tell the difference between his work and a real Banksy's. He had total distain for him. He told me you could put his work up against Banksy's and there are very few people, expert or otherwise, who could tell the difference."

Adam couldn't judge whether Horace was having a meltdown or had just totally lost the plot. Either way, it didn't really matter because, at this point, Jean piped up. "Well, I don't think you've just told us anything we didn't know already, but (holding up her phone) it's nice to have it all recorded and saved for posterity."

"And I think we have enough to take things from here!" Sergeant Greig, flanked by officers Turcat and Trubshaw, appeared through the trees and, sideling past Jean, Rupert, Dylan and Adam, made their way to Horace's side.

For the third time in as many minutes, Horace's eyes had widened. And, if it were at all possible, his jaw had also dropped even further towards the ground than before. However, this time his shoulders and head joined in, slumping down and forward in such a way that seemed to make him age twenty or thirty years right in front of them. The eleven days of Christmas had indeed come back to haunt Horace. And he suddenly realised that even an exorcism wasn't going to get him out of this mess.

The two policemen clicked their handcuffs in place, one on each of Horace's wrists. Apparently, neither wanted the other to be able to claim sole responsibility for the collar.

"How nice to see you again, Councillor." purred a voice Horace had not heard for some time. Distracted by the cold metal touching his skin, he hadn't noticed Vicky joining the throng. "For God's sake!" he shouted in Adam's general direction. "Have you invited the whole of Lancaster to drop by and gawp at this little production of yours? Let's have a party, why don't we."

Vicky looked him straight in the eyes and said, "I didn't need an invitation. I wouldn't have missed this for the world. You took me for a fool and made me look an idiot. Nearly cost me my job. But there's no need for you to worry about that now. Because, Councillor, tonight, me and our little group of merry men and women here will be packing up any sorrows we had and toasting your demise. We're going to have one hell of a shindig." She stepped towards the prisoner until he was within touching distance. "Dreadfully sorry, Horace." She began lightly slapping his cheeks, a la Eric Morcombe, while saying through very pouted lips, "I'm afraid it's one you won't be able to attend".

Horace wondered, if he hadn't been under restraint, whether he'd have succumbed to the sudden urge he had to punch the insurance woman in the mouth. But while he was considering on exactly which side of that conundrum he might have come down, he heard a man's voice coming from somewhere behind him. "Can I have an invite to the party?" Turcat and Trubshaw were restricting Councillor Board's ability to turn, but soon the owner of the question walked past him and into view.

Horace didn't recognise the man and, given the way he looked and how he was dressed, he was sure, if they had ever met, that he would have remembered him. He had on a donkey jacket, unbuttoned and flapping open, revealing a Nero collar style shirt of red and green hoops. Topping this all off was a mop of bright orange hair, cut in a style more associated with the 1960s.

While trying to take in this sight, he heard a second voice. "I'd appreciate an invitation too, if there's one going." Horace didn't need to wait long before this man also came into view, dressed the same and walking barely two strides behind the first voice but in perfect step with it. He could now see that the two characters were also wearing the same coloured trousers, rolled up two or three inches above the ankle and that both had tartan bags slung over their shoulders and appearing to hold their jackets in place.

"If there's any sort of party in the offing, I trust I'll be allowed in?" questioned a further, identically clad figure who had just wandered into Horace's line of sight.

"And if they're going, I'm going!" were the determined words of what, Horace prayed, would be the final matchingly attired member of whatever gang had just appeared.

All this while, Adam had been trying to remain collected and calm. He was also attempting to give the appearance of someone who knew exactly what was going on. However, admitting to himself that he was completely lost and desperately wanting to understand what really was happening, he sidled up next to Dylan and whispered, "Who the hell are these guys?"

Dylan whispered back that while he thought the idea of putting the blocks back on the wall and hiding them behind the *Big Kid Circus* awning was great, "I thought of calling it operation, *Christmas under Canvass*, by the way," he didn't think he was the best man for the job.

"Rupert told me that before approaching dad to take the Banksy off the wall, Jean had said she'd spoken with a proper building firm." He nodded towards the four men now standing together at the foot of the wall, apparently admiring their handiwork. "He said Jean thought them a decent bunch of guys, but that they hadn't liked the smell of the job, so had declined.

I gave them a call to see if they might be willing to help us out. When I explained what we were doing – and why - they seemed more than happy to be involved. One of the brothers was particularly keen. He said that when they first looked at the job, he knew something wasn't right. That it was despicable an elected official should take advantage of one of his constituents in such a way. He ended by saying he and his brothers would do whatever I asked. They helped me move all the pieces from beneath the round-a-bout last night and worked straight through plastering them all back in place. All in time for our grand opening.

Of course, another reason they helped out might be because I think one of them fancied Jean.

"One of the brothers fancied Jean?" repeated Adam. He felt the nub of a possible story here. "Which one?" Dylan thought for a moment before looking over to the four strangely clad lads at the foot of the wall. "I think it's the good-looking one."

Adam wondered, not for the first time, if Dylan was a little more astute than he sometimes made out, but decided to leave that for another day. Instead, he asked about Jean. "Why have you been avoiding her?"

He said, "As soon as Rupert came back from meeting her, I could see it in his eyes. Rupert loved Jean. But I didn't know if Jean loved Rupert. Or if she was Horace's mole, or something."

Adam asked if he meant that Jean might be his moll, but Dylan just said no. "Although I was worried she might be working underground or something." Adam thought he'd leave that comment for another day as well and let him continue.

"In the end, I thought it best not to say anything to anyone about giving her the envelope, nor that I even knew who she was. If the police started to think she was involved in Horace's scheme, they might take her away from Rupert. And Rupert loves Jean. And I wouldn't want to make Rupert sad."

Dylan returned his gaze to the wall and the brothers. I thought of calling it *Operation Grand Opening*." Adam let Dylan drift off, back into his own little world for a bit. He returned to reality not long after and said, "I told them that Rupert loves Jean. They said they were happy for him. Even the attractive one. They're nice guys, really. I think they might even be living the dream."

Chapter 39

The following week, Adam was sitting at the desk as far away from the naughty corner as one could possibly imagine. Actually, *sitting* is not the best description; he was leaning back on the chair with his feet crossed and resting up on the desk. His EarPods were in, Steve Harley's *Make me smile (come up and see me)* was blaring through them and all was well with his world. The report showing the latest circulation figures for overall newspaper distribution in the greater Lancaster area was lying on his desk. Not only was his newspaper at the top of the list, but the competing rags had sold too few copies to make a statistical comparison possible.

His scoop, *COUNCILLOR, NOT ABOVE BOARD AFTERALL,* had taken the town by storm and the story was so strong it had been running for days. That headline on the front page was his. The name above the fold, also his. The name of the person for whom life, at this very moment, was great, Adam Nicola.

The Lancaster Star had splashed his copy across eight pages, and it covered every single one of Horace's exploits. From the gambling debts, to doctoring the Council's books. From coercing an innocent and vulnerable young man into creating a mural on his garden wall, to devising an insurance scam of glacial magnitude. Adam had even included a section on the Councillor breaking, entering and stealing from his neighbour's homes, and then framing a wholly innocent and upstanding member of the community with robbery.

He had written and rewritten this last section of his story dealing with Gazza's involvement a number of times. On balance, Adam decided the most likely alternative slant of, *local wide boy nearly gets what's coming to him*, was, after everything Gazza had been through, perhaps a touch harsh. And anyway, holding up Mr G Danot as one of Lancaster's own and someone who had been much scorned made for more sympathetic reading. Not to mention better circulation (although, much to Adam's total delight, that is exactly what Ffion had been talking about constantly for the past couple of days).

Adam glanced at the report on his desk and reflected on the phrase *better circulation*. It was really a coded message to every corner shop owner in the city: 'You better quadruple, septuple, or even octuple the copies of *The Star* you usually stack on your shelves, and while you're at it, cancel the orders of any rival publication. Because every one of your customers wants to read about the demise of their local Councillor. And it ain't in anybody else's paper other than ours.'

He had started his story in fairly traditional style, covering the who, why, where, when and how of the whole saga. But while that served well for the journalistic purists, such prose rarely led to a surge in sales figures. The people of Lancaster wanted the grime and the gossip beneath the facts. They craved the unimaginable. Were desperate to read the incredible. They wanted the sex and the crime.

And so, even if it was only in the noble cause of boosting sales, Adam felt it was his duty to try and give it all to them. Of course, that required a few modest embellishments of the truth, or fabrications, as they are known on Fleet Street. But, as Adam had proven time and time again, he wasn't proud. He was happy to give the public whatever they wanted. And in spades.

To beef up Horace's rather bland persona, he threw in suggestions of spurned lovers and failed marriages. He also highlighted that the police had not ruled out the possibility of machetes or samurai swords being involved in the burglaries. The fact they hadn't even considered ruling them in went unmentioned.

Adam reminded his readers that the subject matter of the extraordinary mural had a religious angle, thereby enabling him to toss in the possibility it had been encouraged by some of the more liberal wing of the local clergy. He even mentioned that while Horace's betting addiction had been central to every step he had taken over the last year, it didn't stop Adam from letting slip the suggestion that terrorism might also have played its part in the whole sorry saga.

Everyone in the city and beyond talked of nothing else for days. But once the speculation had subsided and the salacious titbits exhausted, focus began to fall on the massive amount of Council money Horace had embezzled. And no surprise, therefore, the tax-paying residents of Lancaster soon began asking questions as to the effect and impact of the Council losing nearly half a million pounds of *their* money might have on *their* local tax bills.

As it happens, there was no cause for concern. Luckily for them, Adam Nicola, intrepid reporter and calmer of troubles, was on hand and on their side. For it was he, and he alone, as he wasted no time, space, or energy in telling his dear readers, who could bring them good news on this subject.

In a specially composed editorial, Adam first confirmed everyone's fears that Gill, Wills, James, Farr & Andrews had indeed paid out their £5 million to Horace and that the money was already long gone.

He then built up the tension, saying that much of the cash had vanished into the black holes of the payday loan companies to whom Horace had been in debt. And he kept his readers on tenterhooks, wondering their fate, as he wandered off piste with details of how these firms operated before finally returning to the matter at hand. In bold letters, three-quarters of the way below the fold, he announced *THE STAR FINDS COUNCIL CASH*. What actually happened was that before settling his debts with Wonga Wonga Wonga.com and the likes, Councillor Board had broken the habit of his recent lifetime and done the decent thing: replenishing the Council's depleted deposit account. The fact that, on close inspection, it was clear this had nothing whatsoever to do with *The Star's* intervention was simply glossed over. The Council's accounts were in balance and the newspaper was able to scream from the headlines, *'YOU HEARD IT HERE FIRST, FOLKS'*.

Having saved the inhabitants of Lancaster from financial disaster, Adam brashly went on to confirm, '....in an exclusive interview with Senior UK Vice President, Vicky Dunaway', even more good news. With the "Banksy," or at least the vast majority of it, now back in its rightful place on the wall, he informed his public at large that the insurance company had withdrawn its lawsuit against the Council for multimillion pounds in reparation.

This was primarily because the story of the 11 Days of Christmas had spread so far and so wide that the mural had effectively doubled its value. As GWJF&A technically owned the painting, it was itself now quids in, making it easy for them to play the role of virtuous benefactor.

The American owners of Gill, Wills, James, Farr & Andrews were more than happy with the publicity (and the net £5 million added to their balance sheet) and therefore decided it was best all round to let matters lie as they currently lay.

Adam concluded his piece with tales of local interest, affecting local people. The sort of stuff on which regional newspapers thrive.

He wrote more expansively about Victoria Dunnaway. How she had recently relocated to the county town and been promoted to Senior Vice President, exotic artworks. And how she'd announced her firm would be paying out rewards of £5000 each to a number of very special local people, "......without whom such a successful outcome in the whole dreadful affair would not have been achieved."

He introduced his readers to the touching story of Jean and Rupert. How they had been thrown together by circumstance and were now planning a wedding ceremony to take place in the park, near the spot where they met.

Adam waxed lyrical about the contributions of Colin, Colin, Colin and Colin. How they had skilfully avoided becoming embroiled in Horace's schemes and instead restored what had become, in barely a matter of days, a City treasure to its rightful place. His piece also mentioned that Colin & Sons were available for all your building and demolition needs.

There was, needless to say, a prominent piece on *Local Renaissance Man*, Dylan Danot, as he insisted Adam describe him. Few who read the full story about the white van that turned green, the *red letter day* delivery, Jasper Carrot, and the involvement of the town's round-a-bout, ended up with much of an idea how any of it had impacted on events at all. But that didn't seem to matter. It was a good read and it sported a great photo of Dylan with his thumbs up, looking somewhat gormless yet with a strangely contented glare into the camera. He was surrounded by an eclectic mix. According to the picture's caption, there was his mother, Flo, or Florence for long; his brothers Brian and Dougal; and a woman identified simply as *Town Council employee*. It wasn't immediately apparent how this young lady fitted into all this, but Dylan was adamant. "I refuse to have the photo taken without her. So, taken with her in it, it was. Once the shot was complete, Adam watched the two of them walk arm in arm across the square. Dylan had avoided all his questions about where or when they met. Adam had one last try, shouting out, "Who are you?"

Dylan shouted back, "I'm Dylan. Some of my friends call me Bob, though I'm really not too sure why."

Adam yelled back, "No. Not you. Dylan. The woman by your side. Who are you? And what are you doing?"

The young lady on Bob/Dylan's arm looked over her shoulder and, in a rich Ukrainian accent, purred, "My name is Ira. And unless I am very much mistaken, my guess is that we're going to be living the dream." She paused for a moment before adding, "But then, as I am, Miss Taken, who knows what we're going to do? Maybe we'll just hang out at this round-a-bout."

As they disappeared from view behind the rabbit and the horse, Adam decided he'd have to leave their story for another day. He still had to conclude the whole narrative of events with details of what happened to Gazza and Paul.

Not long after the story had been published, Paul's conviction was quashed. It seems that being commissioned by the owner to paint his wall and stumbling across stolen goods in a park are yet to be made criminal offences in the UK and he was granted his freedom in fairly quick time. There was not, however, to be any form of compensation coming his way. The Home Secretary of the day was famously against letting anything like a person's innocence stand in the way of locking them up, so she blocked all and any moves by the local people of Lancaster to grant Paul reparation. To her credit, or perhaps to try and stop the negative story about her running in the press, she did ensure the whole process was concluded with uncharacteristic speed. The governor and duty officers of HMP Stafford were ordered to put their festive celebrations on hold and come into work on 26th December so that Prisoner 090256 could be let out the moment his release papers were signed.

Paul's actual departure from incarceration was characteristically low-key.

He'd said very little throughout his time in prison as it was, so it was perhaps no surprise that he decided to leave at the crack of dawn without fanfare or a welcoming out committee. Warden Wardon was the warden on duty, seeing him safely off the premises. He'd just popped the back end of a Gregg's sausage roll he'd found at the bottom of an inside pocket of his tunic when Paul presented himself for release. Still, he managed a reasonably coherent, "Fair play to you, son. All the best." while polishing it off.

Not long after Paul had first been sentenced, the guards had put a poster of Banksy's mural of a prisoner escaping from Reading Gaol in his cell, a la *Shawshank Redemption*. Whether this had been done as an act of kindness, with the aim of brightening up his accommodation, or a somewhat crueller objective to leave their new charge in now doubt exactly where here was, who could say. But whatever the intention, shortly after Paul had vacated the premises, they found he had left them a wee gift of his own.

It was around the time that Warden Wardon had waved goodbye to Prisoner 090256 and wiped the pastry crumbs from his sleeve that the process of clearing out Paul's cell, ready for the next inhabitant, had begun. The three officers tasked with the job were not expecting it to eat too much into their day. Mr Gunningham had taken the paints and brushes he'd been permitted with him and, as far as they could see, had left no other belongings behind. However, any thought of a quick whisk round with a broom and then straight down to the mess for a well-earned brew was dismissed the moment they removed the poster.

Hidden beneath and beautifully crafted on the bare brick wall was what, at first glance, appeared to be the painting of a rather twee farmyard scene; the sort you'd see on a ranch in America's mid-west with a funny-shaped barn in the background, surrounded by horizontal wood fencing. In the foreground was a pig, sitting on some form of commode and wearing a bicorne hat adorned with little white arrows. In the background, looking at him from over the fence, were a number of animals. On closer inspection, the creatures had been given strange, indeed human, features. "That cow looks a bit like you, Alice." said one of the guards, pointing towards the large beast on the left of the artwork. "Better that than a donkey who's got your nose." she responded, pointing to the animal a little further to the right. The third officer thought he'd lay claim to the cockerel, strutting around just inside the fencing. "More like a useless capon." ventured Alice.

News of *Banksy's Farm* spread quickly and everyone, including the governor, wanted to see it for themselves. Those due to be incarcerated in this cell on that day were found alternative accommodation. This enabled all those able and permitted to move around freely to get to look over, admire and, if the cap fitted, take ownership of the mural.

Adam wondered whether Paul had ever found out, or indeed anticipated, the love and passion with which his gaolers embraced his work. Or whether any of them worked out, or even considered, whether the artist had intended to be cruel or kind.

By contrast, Prisoner 190255 wasn't planning to leave his constraints without first trying to organise ceremony or pomp.

In recognition of Adam's support, Gazza had given *The Star* exclusive newspaper rights to his story and indeed, it was their reporter who met him at the prison gates on his release. Adam told him he wanted to ensure the first face Gazza saw on the outside was a friendly one; though he didn't feel it necessary to mention he also wanted to make absolutely sure that no one else could muscle in on his exclusive newspaper rights.

He persuaded Ffion to stump up for first-class train tickets back home and in the more relaxed and spacious environment of the carriages towards the rear of the train, Adam took the opportunity to get started on the story. It proved not to be the most complex interview he'd ever conducted. He'd barely placed his journalist's *Dictaphone* on the table and pressed the record button before Gazza launched into a rant to end or trump all tirades.

Adam had covered everything he needed to know about events leading up to his conviction from their last meeting in prison. What he was hoping for, over optimistically as it was turning out, was perhaps a philosophical view on life inside for an innocent man. What he got, however, was an hour's worth of bile and vitriol directed towards the police, the judiciary and the government. Even the king came in for a little bit of a bashing.

As they pulled into Lancaster station, Adam was resolved to work with what he'd been given. He made his excuses and took a taxi straight to the office. Given that *The Star's* loyal readership were largely proud working-class royalists and the minor issue that Charles III had only been on the throne for a handful of minutes, he decided to dampen down (edit out completely) any mention of the monarch in Gazza's tale. As it happened, the changes to his copy weren't going to stop there. Adam had toned down much of Gazza's rant, put it into more gentle and sensible prose and emailed it to him to cast an eye over. A couple of days later, he was given a message to call a Mr Danot.

As soon as he managed to track him down, it became clear that Gazza had had second thoughts about casting mass aspersions on the British judiciary system. Indeed, he asked Adam if he wouldn't mind reworking his entire piece to include his heartfelt thanks to the group he described as "the powers that be" for the kind and considerate way in which they had treated him throughout this unfortunate situation.

Adam cobbled something together that seemed to tell the tale in the rather bland and unexciting way Gazza had now requested, while still trying to make it spicy enough to keep the public interest alive. But he remained confused as to why Gazza had been so keen to turn the tale he'd relayed on the train completely upside down.

It was sometime later that he was to discover the truth. Apparently, shortly after Adam had left him at Lancaster station, Sergeant Greig had paid Gazza a visit. He was sympathetic to Gazza's situation and apologetic for any role he or the force may have had to play in his incorrect incarceration. But he also ensured Mr Danot was left in no doubt that the police were well aware of his other various dubious exploits and activities. If Gazza was prepared to tone down any attack he might have been considering making about the police's conduct in this unfortunate affair, he would close the book on any current lines of inquiry he may, or may not, be conducting. A very quo pro quid arrangement that Gazza seemed all too happy to accept.

Adam uncrossed his legs and sat back upright in his chair. He scrumpled up the circulation report and tossed it into the bin, thinking on Bradley Meaner's words as he did so. "In the newspaper business, you are only as good as your last story." He wondered if Ffion would have gotten along with old Mr Meaner. She's never satisfied either, he thought. Which was probably one of the reasons he respected her so much.

But now was not the time to dwell on the sayings of past university dons or the whims of current employers. He'd delivered on a promise and now it was time to collect. The news story he'd put together may well have exposed an embezzler, saved the city's finances and overturned two miscarriages of justice. But it had also told the tale of a beleaguered American insurance company and the magnificent role their UK-based Senior Vice President had played. He had a dinner reservation to make. For two.

Chapter 40

The 28th of December. The fourth day of Christmas.

Two men are in Ryelands Park, sitting on Dennis's bench and discussing, at length, Adam's piece in the newspaper. One of them had his feet up, resting on a large blue and amber rucksack.

The police have cleared away almost all evidence that anything troublesome had ever happened in the vicinity. The spot where the bag with the stolen goods was found had been covered over. The grasses flattened down by the various items of kitchenalia that had once laid nearby were now pointing skyward. The circus tarpaulin had been taken back into store and nearly all the blue and white *DO NOT CROSS* tape had been removed. Only a stubborn strip, reading *DO NO* remained, caught and just out of reach in the middle of one of the nearby bushes.

The younger of the two suddenly stood up, sweeping his arm in the general direction of the large, imposing mural on the boundary wall behind them. Paul Gunningham said, "And this is it." This is what all the trouble was about."

The other man followed Paul's lead and got to his feet. He was clearly the senior of the two, although the age differential was far from the most striking thing about them. Despite his age, the older man had a thick head of shocking blonde hair, with red, green and blue tints at the sides. He also sported two golden hooped earrings.

Tim Linquist spent some time taking in the full effects of the work before him. He marvelled at the artwork, the brush strokes and spraying technique. "I particularly like the way you play with the mind of anyone looking at the piece. Everyone can see it relates to the gifts in the *Twelve Days of Christmas* song, but some of the days are a little more, shall we say, subtle than others. I mean, just starting at the beginning...." Tim began to sing the tune, "On the first day of Christmas, my true love gave to me.....a one-man band with eyes of deep azure?

It doesn't even rhyme, let alone scan."

Paul said, "That's because you've got it all wrong. A chap called Don Partridge was a busker in the sixties. He had a huge hit with a song called *Blue Eyes*. I just liked the idea that on the first day of Christmas, my true love might give to me," and here Paul picked up the tune, '*Don Partridge's latest LP*'."

Tim had the look of someone not sure whether they'd just been shown a grain of genius, or a pile of pretentious piffle.

Paul, sensing that he had not even managed to whelm his audience, said, "Perhaps I better take you through the others." and shepherded Tim closer to the wall.

"The second and third days are fairly obvious." He glanced at Tim, hoping for at least a modicum of agreement. When none was forthcoming, he continued anyway. "The *YEEZY BOOST 350* trainers: a classic since they were first sold in 2022, are known as Turtle Doves." Paul paused again, but Tim was just staring back blankly. "Well, there's two of them...Two Turtle Doves!"

Tim frowned. Then smiled. And finally nodded in recognition. The penny had dropped. "And these three dogs," he said to Paul, "standing in front of the Eiffel Tower. They're French. Three French chiens. Brilliant."

The area in the bottom right-hand corner stuck out like the proverbial. One of the Colins, no one was quite sure which, had filled the gap with a blank slab, the original having been smashed by one of Horace's elephants. He'd done his best to make the best of a bad job, but the colour and activity elsewhere on the wall merely highlighted its absence of anything.

Tim saw Paul looking lovingly at the empty tile and tried to distract him. Moving up a row, he pointed to number 5 and started to think out loud. "Snow, igloo. A refrigerator and an ice cream cone. They're all white? No, there's a pint of lager here. That's yellow." He looked at Paul. "You know, I could do with a nice cold pint of......." Tim had a sudden epiphany. "Cold. They're all cold. These are five cold things!"

Paul grinned with self-satisfaction.

Tim didn't notice. He was enjoying the game. "Now number 6. Number 6. No, I'll come back to this one, because I've seen that your seventh day of Christmas has some people in the river beneath the *Morfa bridge*. These are seven Swansea swimmers."

Moving slightly to his right, he stroked the nose of one of the eight cows with his index finger. "No. We'll have to come back to that one too. But the next day looks a tad more straightforward. These are nine ladybirds dancing. Nice brush work." Paul blushed. "And these ten members of the MCC are obviously Lords. Leaping." The eleventh slab, with its eleven crisp packets, required a bit of thought. But not, as it turned out, all that much. Over the years, Tim had spent a fair amount of time bird watching in Anglesey, always staying in the Prince of Wales Arms. It was close to the island's bird sanctuary; their price was reasonable and the beer pretty good. The one criticism he had was they didn't do any food. The only edible items they had for sale behind the bar were crisps. Pipers crisps. He'd cursed them many a time on many occasions in Moelfre. But today, in Lancaster, they proved to be the key he needed to the eleventh day of Christmas. There were eleven pipers. Not actually piping, but pipers, nonetheless.

Tim took out a white handkerchief and waved it in mock surrender. "I have to give up on these last three. You'll need to walk me through them." he said, with a trace of failure in his voice.

Paul pointed out that the slab in the top right hand corner contained twelve rings, or 'Os' with stars: "Twelve Ring O Stars. The Beatles' drummer." He then dipped down to the even numbers in the middle row. Touching the edge of number six, he said, "I was trying to generate an east-end gang war concept here, with half a dozen *geezers laying* into some poor sod. But as to this one..." Paul hit the eighth slab with the side of his fist. "I'm not surprised you couldn't unravel it. I'm guessing your French is not that good?" Tim sort of shrugged. "They call the mathematical equals sign *au pairs*. I suppose it kind of makes sense. Anyway, I thought eight au pairs, or maids, each with a cow, could be eight maids a milking!"

Having unlocked the meaning behind the eleven days of Christmas that remained on the wall, the two men took a few paces back. They both stood in silence, admiring the work looking down on them.

Tim broke the peace. "Impressive." he said. "Extraordinary. Brilliant conceptual artwork. I just love it." And then, slightly more hesitantly, "Of course, some of the days are better than others, but still. Mighty impressive. But," pointing towards the bottom right corner, "such a shame about the gap."

Paul slightly self-depreciatingly said, "Well, the Tweety-pie thing.........was not perhaps the greatest idea I ever had, but I was really short of time and" he added slightly sheepishly, "...it sort of worked. Sort of." After another thoughtful pause, he added, "I wonder whether I should repaint it. Put the cartoon characters back in. That would at least be better than the blank square we're left with at the moment."

The two men stood in silence. Both were clearly considering the issue. Paul put his hand on Tim's shoulder. "You know, when I heard about the four builders who slaved away for nothing to put the eleven of my remaining slabs back on the wall, just to spite Horace – and that they even added in a blank one where the number four had been - my faith in human nature was restored." He drifted away again, reflecting on his words. "Fugl was their name." he said. "Everyone thought they were the Smith brothers, but no. Their real name was Fugl." Then he added, "It's quite an unusual name, don't you think?"

"Not where I come from." said Tim. "It's actually quite a common surname in Scandinavia. In Helsinki, we say lintu. But in Norway, Denmark and Iceland, it's fugl. The translation is *bird*. We even have rhymes and folk laws about the little things. I remember my mother sending me to bed with her favourite tale. 'Pick up a fugl and put it in your palm; blow in its ear and it will give you all the luck you deserve.' It doesn't rhyme or scan as well in English as it does in Finnish, but you get the idea."

"Well, whether they are Fugls or Smiths, they certainly helped me out." said Paul.

Tim opened his mouth as if to continue the discussion, but instead held up his hand and stared into the distance. He started mumbling various things to himself and then suddenly got quite agitated - no, excited. He pushed past Paul, picking up the backpack of painting tricks as he went. "Do you mind?" he asked Paul, pointing towards the blank square in the bottom right-hand corner. Paul simply shrugged and said, "Be my guest."

Tim ran to the foot of the wall and within moments he was painting furiously.

He began sketching out a scene that involved four men.

They were of similar height and were all dressed identically: collarless shirts of green with red hoops beneath Donkey jackets, blue and unbuttoned. They wore corduroy khaki trousers with turn-ups and Dr Martin boots, each one of the eight toe caps stained with what looked like dried cement. All four of them were carrying tartan bags slung over their shoulders, with the strap diagonally across the chest holding the jackets in place and giving the appearance that they were each sporting a military sash. Each man had a dramatic shock of deep amber hair, cut in a style *The Beatles* would have been proud of.

Tim laid the brushes and paints on the grass and took a few paces back to stand at Paul's side. The two men looked in silence at the now completed scene before them.

Paul was struck by how well this final, twelfth square fitted in with the other eleven. He had only met Tim for the first time that morning at the train station. The stranger had gotten in touch, saying he was an old friend of Adam Nicola who had stumbled across his article online. He said, "I absolutely just *have* to see you. Urgently!"

Now standing here in the park, Paul couldn't explain the deep kindred spirit and connection he suddenly felt for someone he'd never even heard of a few hours ago.

Turning to Tim, he said, "Your style and touch are very similar to my own. People have told me that my work is indistinguishable from Banky's. I'm not sure many people looking at this work for the first time could tell which was the *odd day out*, so to speak. Any one of these slabs could have been painted by either of us. Or, I suppose, the man himself?"

He waited for Tim to pick up the conversation and react to the question he'd left hanging. But Tim said nothing.

After a few moments, Paul accepted he was not going to hear any more on the subject and changed tack. "So, this is just a scene involving four guys named Colin?"

Tim explained, "Yes, but not *just* Colin." He started humming a tune unfamiliar to Paul, although he had heard the words before. Tim was singing, 'Pick up a fugl and put it in your palm; blow in its ear and it will give you all the luck you deserve.'

He looked up at Paul and then, turning back to the painting he had just completed, spoke directly to it. "Well, there you all are. In your rightful place between five gold rings and three French hens. The Fugl brothers. Or, as we'd say in English, Four Colin Birds.